THE SOUR CREEK RAID

When Billy Brett came upon Abel Crane, he took him to Sam Yorke's camp where preparations for a railroad robbery were under way. Complications arose when word was received that the legendary Marshal Stoddart was after Crane, but Yorke and his men decided the carefully planned raid at Sour Creek would still take place. Yet nothing was quite as it seemed and the outlaws were in for a few surprises. In the end death was the only certainty.

THE SOUR CREEK RAID

THE SOUR CREEK RAID

by

Lee F. Gregson

Dales Large Print Books
Long Preston, North Yorkshire,
England.

British Library Cataloguing in Publication Data.

Gregson, Lee F.
    The Sour Creek raid.

A catalogue record for this book is
available from the British Library

ISBN 1-85389-942-9 pbk

First published in Great Britain by Robert Hale Limited, 1998

Copyright © 1998 by Lee F. Gregson

Cover illustration © Faba by arrangement with Norma
Editorial S.A.

The right of Lee F. Gregson to be identified as the author
of this work has been asserted by him in accordance with
the Copyright, Designs and Patents Act, 1988

Published in Large Print 1999 by arrangement with Robert
Hale Ltd.

Dales Large Print is an imprint of
Library Magna Books Ltd.
Printed and bound in Great Britain by
T.J. International Ltd., Cornwall, PL28 8RW.

One

Bob Teech had come sniffing again in more ways than one when he had got her message. But she sure had some questions of her own. Lola Barrett: no beauty, but a real handsome woman. Nobody's fool. Teech knew better than to take her for one; which did not mean he was about to tell her the whole story, right off.

She had put on her blue robe and she slid deftly away now when he reached a hand out and went to the single window that gave a view over another roof, a livery and corral. She raised the sun-cracked shade a few more inches. Still lying among rumpled bedclothes, Teech stared at her back, his long, sallow face with its fair, wispy moustache very still. Once she took

7

a certain mindset, you could not push this woman. Teech's history, as far as women were concerned, was far from good, yet he had come to know that this one was not afraid of him. And not backward in questioning him and challenging him if the need seemed to be upon her, as it was now.

'If somethin' goes wrong, how the hell do I know it won't come back on me? Will it be me that's left with my neck stickin' out?' She was still turned away from him, the robe pulled tight around her full-curved body by her folded arms. The very set of her was telling him that, at this late stage, she half regretted this, regretted getting so far in. This was Teech's third visit in a short period of time. Maybe she was thinking that now she had delivered the firm information he had been seeking, he would cut free and not keep his word, leaving her with unmanageable risks. She was sure as hell giving him that impression. Teech continued appreciating the subtleties of soft curves beneath the blue robe, the slim line of her neck, the grabbed-together hang of her black hair, measuring the full length to her buttocks.

He said, 'There's goddamn' risks for all of us, come to that.'

She wasted no time jumping on the *all*. 'That's another thing. Who's *all?*' She meant maybe Billy Brett, mostly.

'Cain't git it done on my lonesome, Lola.'

Now she did turn her head to look at him, but remained standing at the grimy window. 'Billy Brett's on the move, you say?'

'He is.'

'Billy an' how many more, Bob? Two? Three? Jack Geller. Who else?'

'Reb Stone.'

She had turned her face away again. 'You, Billy, Geller, Stone. That's all? You mean that's all there are with Billy? Where's the other one, Bob? Where's Sam Yorke? I thought this was all about Sam.'

'Sam, he'll come in soon as he knows the word's good.'

'So he *is* back? No doubt?'

Teech shifted, swung his legs over the side of the bed, reaching for his shirt. 'Sam'll be there when he's wanted.' He could tell by the turn things had taken and her tone of voice that she had no intention of getting back in the bed. Now she started going over the names again.

'You, Billy Brett, Jack Geller, Reb Stone, Sam Yorke. Five.'

'That's it.' He thought it best not to mention the possibility of Yorke bringing the brawler, Rudy Goss.

'That's not exactly it, Bob. There's me. As far as the split goes, that's six.'

'Yuh'll git your cut,' Teech said. 'That I guarantee.'

'Yeah? You make the promises for Sam Yorke now?'

'Cain't do no more'n say it. Yuh got to take it on trust, like I got to take this word o' yourn on trust.'

10

She was rubbing her wrapped-around hands, very slim hands, on her upper arms. 'The word come direct from Seligman, nobody else.'

'Here?' Maybe he meant not only this town but this particular room. This bed.

'No. In Garrick. Christ, I wouldn't lead 'im here.'

He was all but fully dressed, looking for his left boot. 'But does Seligman know yuh've come here?'

'My comin's an' goin's are none of his business. If he knows anything by now, it's that.' Teech was aware that she knew a lot of men, and he would have no idea who half of them were. Still, he had to get to know more about the information she had given him. Billy Brett would be poking and prying, asking questions. But Yorke would be the one who would demand all details. There was too much at stake for Sam Yorke to go out on a limb on some half-baked word from Lola Barrett or anybody else.

She had come away from the window and was at a closet, lifting clothes out.

Teech said, 'Seligman was takin' one hell of a risk, talkin' about it.'

She glanced at him, her full lips slightly parted. Almost a smile. 'Not quite. There's been kinda ... developments 'tween me an' Bart. Sure you want to know about that?' When he paused in dragging the second boot on, she said, 'Says he wants me to meet 'im in Fort Ross. Right after he gets this job done.' When Teech's narrow mouth fell open she did smile. 'Claims he wants to make an honest woman out o' me. Now, what d'you think about that, Bob? Thing is, I never had a better offer. Not even from present company.'

When he could get it out, he said, 'Jesus. An' that's what you're gonna do?'

She laughed, a pleasant sound, holding a blue dress up in front of her for his inspection. 'What do *you* think, Bob?' It was unclear whether she meant the dress or the news of Bart Seligman's proposal.

'What I hope is, yuh told that fancy asshole where to go!'

Lola raised her delicate, dark brows in mock surprise. 'What? An' have to watch 'im drag his pants on an' go stompin' out, an' maybe next day have second thoughts about what he'd blabbed to me? That'd be real smart, Bob.'

Teech, somewhat deflated, said, 'Jesus, Lola ...'

'What?'

'Never can tell when you're serious.'

'You can take me serious about this shipment, Bob. I'll tell you this, I've never felt surer.'

'How drunk was the bastard?' This was rich, coming from Teech. Maybe she thought so too, for she slid him a half-amused look.

'Sure, ol' Bart's at it again. Comes back worse every time, seems to me. When he gets that way he wants to impress me. Important man. Trusted. Trusted by railroads. Now, ain't *that* somethin'? Like bein' trusted by Beelzebub, no less.' Then she was serious again. 'Wherever Sam Yorke is, wherever Billy Brett is, there's always men dead. They go together.'

'Yuh 'feared fer Seligman's hide, that what it is?'

'No, I'm not.'

'Still got to be sure this word's good. Billy, for one, he'd take it real unkindly if it wasn't.'

'Billy Brett's a madman.'

He wanted to be sure she was getting the message. 'This here ain't no way gonna be no take-your-partners.' Teech was standing at the foot of the bed and had taken up shellbelt, holster and pistol (a Walker .44 Colt) and was putting it on. Standing, he looked skinny enough for it to slip down over his hips. He said, 'An' that brings me to the next part. Seligman ain't gonna be on that train all on his own. How many more?'

'Bart didn't come right out an' say. It

sounded to me like there'd be but one other.'

Teech's expression was not easily read-able. 'Give this here feller a name, did he?'

Lola shook her head. She was standing in front of a dull mirror over the dresser, brushing her long hair while watching Teech in the glass. 'No.' Then, 'Why the hell would he?'

Teech completed the job of thonging the oily holster against his right thigh, straightened and thumbed the hammer-thong in place. 'Two don't seem near enough if all the other stuff's true.'

She had the black hair cast down in front of her left shoulder and was busy braiding it into a single, heavy cable. 'I thought about it,' she said. 'What if they had four, five men aboard, all prowlin' up an' down at the Garrick depot? Might as well carry a big sign with how much they got on board. That could bring more blowflies than a week dead horse.'

Teech thought about it for a while. It

15

did make some sort of sense. Finally, he said, 'Yeah ... mebbe so, at that.'

Lola finished making the long, thick braid and coiled it and was now pinning it up at the back. 'When are you gonna stop lookin' for holes in it, Bob?'

'When I'm goddamn' sure I ain't gonna find none.'

'You mean when you're sure Sam Yorke won't.' She turned from the mirror to find Teech scowling at her.

'Yuh got somethin' of a mouth on yuh, Lola. Allers did have.'

'It's told *you* all you wanted to know. Christ, Bob, d'you see me givin' Bart Seligman a checklist o' questions? Sam can't have it all tied up tidy in a bundle. I can't say more. I can't *do* more.'

Teech was still looking sour. Maybe the image of that half-drunk, balding bastard panting away atop Lola Barrett was galling him more than he would have admitted. Them in some better-class room, in Garrick.

'Didn't say yuh could,' he said, sensing, perhaps, that he had pushed her too far. She was still flinty, though, and now gave him something else to chew on.

'After all I've done, maybe Sam Yorke won't risk it.'

Teech went pacing to the window, looking out broodingly across the nearby roof. Dust was lifting. Another hot, grit-whipping day. 'I doubt there's any left standin' who'd risk tryin' to take Sam Yorke. Not now. One or two, mebbe, in all of a thousand mile. Them as didn't take ol' Sam, years back, they're long gone or they're shovin' up sand somewheres. Add in Billy. Who'd be fool enough?'

Stretching her arms, sighing, Lola said, 'Samuel Yorke. The one bad man they never did get. For all the struttin' an' speech-makin', all the fancy marshals an' the posses an' the bountymen. Still, Sam hurt one helluva lot o' folk, Bob.' And rumours about his having reappeared had been wafting on the wind for some while.

But you could never put money on just how substantial such things were.

Teech was uncomfortable with the turn the discussion had taken. Soon, she might start on about how you could never rely on Sam Yorke doing exactly what he said he would do, once he thought he'd started to notice different sign. For Sam, survival was all that mattered. It was the reason he was still alive and that numerous among those who had set out to take him, were not. Anyway, there were one or two questions yet to be asked.

'This here train,' Teech said.

'Yeah?' She was dabbing perfume behind her small ears.

'It's a freight. No other cars?'

'Freight's what Bart said. It was him that used the word, not me.'

That being so, there would be Seligman and, as far as could be ascertained, one other man as well as the train's regular crew; an engineer, a fireman, a freight conductor. Like as not, it would be one of the latest South-westerns with this new-fangled braking system, *Westing-something*. So, no brakies gawping from the tops of the cars. Teech was still some concerned, though. For one thing, it sounded too easy. That might be how Sam Yorke would see it, too. Billy Brett might not be inclined to give it as much thought; but then, Billy always had been a go-in-blazing kind of *hombre*. And, like as not, come out bleeding, thought Teech sourly.

Now he had to ask her, 'What's the chances yuh could git a look at 'em loadin' it?'

'Oh, for Chrissake, Bob, forget it!'' Now she *was* annoyed, colour coming up in her face. 'Never been near before, an' here I am, this one time, come walkin' into the Garrick depot!'

Teech lifted his hands, making damp-ening-down motions. 'Take it easy Lola ... take it easy.'

'All I know is what I've said; the date, the time, the destination. Plenty of time for you to get in place. I've said what he's told me an' now you know as much as I do.'

'He give away a lot.'

'Bob, hear me again: when he starts on that coffin varnish he'll not let up 'till the bottle's dead. Then he wakes up with a head he's got to clutch hold of. Take it or leave it.' Then she asked, 'You'll be back, later?'

'Not 'till it's done with. No point riskin' my face gittin' back to Seligman.'

She was thoughtful, then suddenly came back to what she had been on at him about, earlier. 'A six-way split. It had better be worth it. An' Bob, you relied on me, now I'm relyin' on you: make sure I get my cut, all fair, Sam Yorke or no Sam Yorke.' He knew well enough that she had no liking for Yorke. He also knew that, if it should come to a stand-off between him and Sam Yorke over it, and Billy Brett standing there grinning like a fool, the mad dog, Brett, there could be no certainties.

'Trust me,' Teech said.

'That's what I mean. I got no choice.'

Now, standing in this stale-smelling little room, there was no more that he could say to her, nothing to alter the quizzical look she was giving him. As soon as he left here, heading out southward, the die would be cast, those who were to take part, come shuffling into place, the business set in motion and gathering momentum.

The woman was thinking that all kinds of people took others on trust and that it worked out or it didn't. Unbeknown to herself or to Teech, she had arrived at the same conclusion that he had. There could be no certainties.

Two

A small fire in a ring of smooth stones was crackling and filmy smoke was barely to be seen more than fifty yards away. Jack Geller had seen it, however, and it had been enough to fetch him in to where Billy Brett and Reb Stone were. Well, where only Billy Brett was visible, hunkered down. Reb Stone was behind a clump of wind-tortured brush, but stepped clear of it when Geller was close enough to be recognized. Stone had a Winchester.

Geller, grunting with relief, swung down. Stone laid his rifle aside and went across to set the coffee pot on the cherry heart of the fire. Stretching his cramped limbs, then unsaddling, Geller said to Billy Brett, 'Well, I talked with Sam.'

Billy nodded slowly, watching the unsaddling. The details he wanted would come soon. Dressed much alike, in rough, grey wool shirts with galluses over shoulders, coarse-weave brown pants and studded leather leggings over the top, these men wore ragged bandannas—dark red, all of them—and dented, dusty hats with leather thongs hanging, and boots that were cracked and dusty. The only visible things that had been well kept were their firearms. Billy Brett's pistol was an old, rakish Colt, Stone's a Forehand and Wadsworth, Geller's a Walker Colt; the rifles were all Winchester repeaters. The men did not look much alike.

Billy Brett was of medium height and build, with a face inclined to plumpness, pale stubble around the mouth, and would have appeared nonedescript but for his eyes. They were small and bright and black and when they settled on something or on someone of interest, did not shift easily. Billy smiled often, but the smiles seldom got as far as the black eyes.

Jack Geller was taller than Brett and of heavier build, with dark, unruly hair that near to buried his ears and was bunched at his neck. Reb Stone was skinny and pale-looking, like he had been bled recently and, from a distance, this pallor offered an impression of youth. Closer-to, he could be seen as a man of middle age, with a creviced face and greenish, brown-shot eyes that were constantly on the move.

Geller was squatting, sipping hot coffee out of a tin mug. Dusty and red-eyed, he was best left be until ready to talk. Even Billy Brett would concede him that much. They were travelling light, these three, living off the land; living off whatever could be picked up. *'Don't say no to Billy Brett.'* This was poor country, near desert, full of cactus and thorn brush and full of venomous creatures just like Billy. From time to time, heading northwards, they would come upon sorry-looking communities, a few adobe buildings, skinny animals in pens, chickens pecking around bare earth, baleful women with skirt-clinging children and silent, surly menfolk. Little to be had in places such as these, but what he fancied, Billy would take; bread, meat or women. Or all three. Now he might be on the move with a purpose in mind, but that did not mean that he would not pause, if so inclined, to take his food and his pleasures where he chose. Still his own man. Always would be.

'So,' he said now to Jack Geller, 'yuh talked with Sam.'

'Yeah.'

'On his own?'

'Rudy Goss was there.'

Goss, the lumbering brawler, shiny-bald, muscular, pea-brained, very dangerous. Billy had seen Goss bust a man's back.

'Christ,' Billy said. 'Wonder what clapped-out whorehouse Sam dug Rudy out of.' Then, seriously, 'Sam got it all set up?'

Geller shook his head. 'Not yet. He's expectin' Bob Teech back any time now.

Reckons it'll be set up then, fer sure.'

'Hopes.'

'Seemed settled in his mind about it. Waitin' fer details is what he said.'

'By Christ,' Billy said, 'somebody better be settled on *somethin'! Me, I ain't haulin' my ass a hunnert an' fifty mile on no pig in a poke!' He rose from his squatting posture, knee joints cracking, and began walking up and down. 'He reckoned it was gonna be worth it. Well, I'm comin'.' Geller had known that his message might provoke something like this. Sam Yorke had said so, too, and had almost chuckled. Well, Sam, chuckling, was not here having to listen to it.

Geller said, 'Way Sam talked, it was sure all on, but Bob Teech had to git the last word. The date. The time.' This did appear to mollify Brett somewhat but the black eyes were alive and in his present mood he could find fault easily, which was the reason Jack Geller was not relishing having to come out with other news, for he knew it would be unsettling. This was something he had got from Yorke, too, but he had only a vague notion of how Yorke had come by it. However, a lot of what passed was by word of mouth, truth, half-truth, whispers, lies, deceits. 'Somethin' else,' Geller said. The way he said it brought Reb Stone closer too. 'There's been a marshal heard of, out after some bastard.'

'A marshal?'

'Yeah. Stoddart.'

That sure brought on-the-move Billy to a stop. *'Stoddart!'* His voice was low but hard. 'Now, what could bring that ague-ridden ol' bastard way south? Who's ass is it he's follerin'?'

'Some bastard called Crane. Abel Crane.'

'Sam knows this?'

'It was Sam told me.'

By God, Sam Yorke would have been as pleased to hear of Stoddart as Billy was. *Ague-ridden* Billy had said. Well, that was as may be. But of all those who had tried, he was the one man who had come close to taking Sam Yorke. Most of that had been down to the fact that it had been very personal between him and Sam.

Reb Stone said, 'Thought that ol' shit would be dead, by this.'

Billy was not smiling. This was indeed unexpected. Billy did not like being taken unawares. He liked to know what cards everybody else was holding. Now, even Sam Yorke—maybe more than anybody— would be casting a few glances over his shoulder. Real bad blood, there was, way back. And there was still good money out for Sam's ears. Not that there were any left, apart from Stoddart, even now, whom Billy Brett would rate a chance of getting to Sam Yorke. So he hoped that Stoddart would soon run down this Abel Crane and get gone from the territory.

It had been at a place a long way from where they were now. Billy Brett had not been there at the time. A young man, Stoddart's son-in-law, had been a county deputy, just starting out. A man had come into town and had got in an argument with some fly boy dealing faro and had buffaloed him and the deputy had been called. The stranger had been Sam Yorke—though not known in that place at that time—and he had been given the word, at the hole-end of a 10-gauge, to get gone and stay gone. Had they but known it, no one would so humiliate Sam Yorke and expect to get clean away with it. During the night, the house, one of several belonging to the county, had been burned to a smoking heap and had burned with it not only the deputy but his young wife as well. Stoddart's girl. That had been the start of Stoddart's setting out after Yorke and coming close to nailing him. Close, but not close enough.

Billy asked, 'Where was he last heard of, Stoddart?'

'A good long ways north,' said Geller. 'Chase River. Thereabouts.'

'An' Sam, what'd he have to say?'

'Like what Reb said. Thought the ol' bastard'd be dead, long since.'

Billy did some more tramping around, scuffing sand. 'Chase River.' Then, 'This Crane. Where's he from? If Stoddart come as far as he has, it's gotta be for some good reason.'

'Dunno. Sam didn't know. He did hear there was somethin' personal.'

'Personal.' Billy repeated the word and stared into distance. Like what was between Stoddart and Sam Yorke was personal. You could not get much more personal than that. But of all the times for Stoddart to come sniffing around, right now was not a good one. Sam in the middle of something. Billy was still squinting into the distance. A small breeze had come up, some dust lifting. It was as though Brett was trying to call upon some other sense, one that might reveal to him some truths about Stoddart and where he had got to and about this man Crane. Some did say old Billy had a touch of Apache blood and that when he kind of let his thoughts drift off in the way he was doing now, the Indian part was showing. So far as was known, nobody had ever asked the question directly. With Billy you never knew how it would be taken. He could laugh one of his odd laughs, or he could just as easily pull the rakish Colt and blow a man's face half off.

'If Stoddart did turn back north, he coulda druv him that way ... On the other hand, if that Crane outfoxed that ol' man, wa-al then, he could be down here still, holed up. What we got to do is keep our eyes peeled. If we come up with that feller, he'd be the man to tell us all there is to know about Stoddart.'

No doubt Geller and Stone as well as Billy Brett had a picture in their minds of a man on the run, probably exhausted, both man and animal, maybe hurt, very wary, apt to let fly at mere shadows. You would do well to take great care in approaching such a man. Whoever this one was, if he had drawn that old dog, Stoddart, such a long distance, then he was not a man to be taken lightly. But the longer he remained at large, the greater the chance that the hunter would return. In the old days, Stoddart had been a mean, persistent bastard. There was no reason to believe that, in his old age, he was any less so.

Jack Geller would have looked to rest up for the remainder of the day, but Billy Brett was still on the move, now thumping a fist into the other palm. *Smack ... smack ... smack.* Behind him, Reb Stone raised his light-coloured eyebrows at Geller. Both of these men had been long enough around Billy to read him, to see that he was in one of his restless, want-to-go-every-which-way moods. To Jack Geller, he said, 'Give yuh a coupla hours, Jack. Take a stretch, git some chow down. Then we're gone from here.'

Geller gave him a look, but nodded, briefly. In Billy's present frame of mind there would be no point in arguing.

Three

Abel Crane was riding hard and not across the kind of terrain he would have chosen in the circumstances. Dusty, brush-strewn flats these were, a long feather of dust pointing the direction of his flight, drawing the bastards like a magnet.

A succession of events had led to this. Well aware that by this time his progress through this particular stretch of country had been clearly marked, he had still considered that a brief visit to a town, Arabella, was worth the risk. He had needed provisions. At first, the signs had looked promising. There was no regular law in Arabella, only an overweight individual employed as a town marshal who, to begin with, had evinced no interest whatsoever in the lone, dusty rider on a bay horse, who had come riding in and visited the mercantile, a place in Arabella that seemed to be everything to everybody.

But Stoddart, of course, had been freely giving out the name and description of the man he was tracking. And Stoddart had been at pains to stress his anxiety to locate Abel Crane just as soon as he could. Wherever there was a telegraph, telegrams had been sent out, far and wide, and the signature, STODDART, US DEPUTY MARSHAL, had naturally caused something of a stir wherever it had been read. If the old but legendary Stoddart wanted this particular man so badly, then, by God, there had to be a real good reason. A dangerous man on the run, here. And though Stoddart's general telegraphing had put no price on Crane, speculation, followed by rumour, had soon taken care of that apparent omission. Mention had been made of $5,000. In time that had become $7,500. Finally, attended by a string of alleged felonies committed in various unspecified places, the price had become $10,000. Word travelled, too, entirely without the aid of the telegraph.

So, remote though this place was, Arabella, his anonymity there was not to endure. By and by, heads were put together and glances were thrown. Finally, the ponderous town marshal, prompted, perhaps unwisely in view of the information that had come in, had hitched at his sagging belt and had challenged Abel Crane.

The tall, rather gaunt man who, in his present dust-caked state, did not look up to much, at least at first glance, had turned slowly from unhitching the bay, to the call of the marshal, a man who had chosen to make his challenge from some sixty feet away. At that point, no support for the marshal had been evident.

What set off the next move seemed not to have anything to do with the man standing with the bay horse. The marshal, who was slung with a pistol, a

Colt Lightning, dragged it from its holster, perhaps merely intending to reinforce the authority of his badge. Crane, however, had not been prepared to test the fat man's reasons and had made at once to mount the bay and put spurs to it, instinctively crouching in the saddle as he did so. Startled, the marshal let fly with the Lightning. Lead did not come within feet of the now urgently riding Crane, but it did spit up dust further along the main street. The marshal shot again, but again the heavy lead flew wide. Crane went hammering out of the dry little town, heading southward. Behind him, encouraged no doubt by the marshal's zeal, other townsmen, fetching out with them a miscellany of firearms, discharged a number of them in the direction of the hard-riding horseman, but, like the marshal's shooting, all to no effect.

That none of this impassioned firing had been returned by Crane must immediately have fed civic enthusiasm to the extent that ten minutes beyond the seedy little settlement, Crane had cast a glance over his shoulder to discover that under rising yellow dust, a posse which must have been frantically got up, was hard on his heels. His horse had been badly in need of freshening, so the attention of these fools now out after him could scarcely have come at a worse time. He had headed out across the only country open to him, these miles and miles of dry flats.

At least one of them was carrying a rifle. Crane heard the lash of it behind him. Though the bullet came nowhere near, the very sound of the weapon caused a prickling of the hair at the back of his neck and he urged the big horse under him to greater effort. One thing was in his favour: at the further edge of the flats was some rougher country of the sort in which he might just manage to throw off his pursuers. Beyond it, however, he believed there lay a further expanse of difficult terrain, a near desert land, and he had no desire to have to push the bay across it and, moreover, fail to locate enough water to sustain himself and the animal. Once among the scarred, low hills ahead of him, however, he had hopes that the riders after him would soon see the risks of his getting into cover and waiting for them and therefore abandon the chase. But he was not going to reach that cover.

To begin with, the bay, strong though it was, began flagging at last. Crane had no option but to allow it to ease down, then bring it to a halt, its sweating, dust-streaked flanks heaving. Seeking as much cover as he could get among the scrappy but razor-armed brush, his rifle now in hand, Crane stood watching the rising dust cloud rapidly coming closer.

As he had expected, the shooting started again from a range that was too great to be effective, as though those doing it needed to hear the guns going off in order to reassure themselves in some way. Crane now levered the Winchester and stood with the butt-plate hard into his right shoulder, waiting. Although now that they were aware that he had stopped, and the pace of the oncoming riders had slackened, he did not have long to wait. Those in the lead, the fat town marshal and a smaller, bearded man, this one carrying a rifle, came into view some fifty yards away. Crane got off a whacking shot, levered and fired again. There was immediate confusion and consternation as the two leading horses knuckled over, pitching their riders to the ground.

Those who were following on went hauling away, left and right, to avoid the downed and rolling men and horses. Calmly, Crane tracked another horse and shot it, the rider being hurled from the saddle as in clouds of dust the animal went down.

Crane remounted and, weaving in and out among the thorn brush, allowed the bay to walk unhurriedly. He kept looking over his shoulder, though, wary of being followed by those four or five who were still mounted, or of being lined up by some rifleman among them. In the event, there was no further pursuit and no more shooting.

When the flats came to an end, still allowing the horse to walk, he entered the rougher, broken country. There were hills covered with little else but dry bunch-grass, but on the summits, a few wind-bent trees. The hills were scarred with numerous clay slips and fissures. Hang-headed though the horse was, it picked its way into a long, shallow valley where there was a stony, dried-up creek. Crane steadily traversed the length of this, up the inclining ground and, at the summit, passed between clay faces and went down a long ochre-coloured slope at the bottom of which lay another stretch of flats which bore only random signs of vegetation and no evidence of other life. Far away to his right, the purple shapes of the Holman Range were drawn against the sky, and Crane knew this was the direction that he must take and that, long before he reached those mountains, he would have passed into a greener, rolling country where some cattle ranches were, and the bright rails of the South-western Railroad gleamed for mile upon mile.

Towards mid-afternoon, having spelled the horse regularly and still allowing it to walk, he came within sight of what, in the heat-haze, looked like a collection of buildings. Crane drew the tired bay to a halt. He ran his tongue between dry, cracked lips, reached for his canteen and, unplugging it, filled his mouth with the last of his sour-tasting water. Nudging the horse, moving on again, he unscabbarded his rifle and levered it. His steady approach through a film of wind-lifted dust was quiet, since the horse was on sandy ground.

What was coming more clearly into view was a group of adobe buildings, a principal one and several outbuildings set around a yard and, nearby, the remains of a couple of corrals. The closer Crane came the more apparent did it become that all of these structures were in very poor shape. Now, only thirty yards out, he saw what clearly was a well with a stone rim about three feet in height.

Crane's senses seemed to be telling him that he had come to a long-abandoned place. Nonetheless he walked the bay around in a wide circle, his eyes probing shadows cast by the afternoon sun. He was seeking evidence of any recent comings and goings. He found no tracks, no horse droppings, no wheel-tracks. It was true that wind-blown dust might well have obliterated some, but tracks made by horses would probably have still been visible, had any been here. He found nothing to arouse his interest. Now he would approach the well.

First, however, Crane dismounted and, leaving the reins trailing—for the bay was too exhausted to go wandering off—he made an inspection of each building, holding the rifle at the hip. Again, nothing, and no one. Only now did he walk to the stone-rimmed well.

A wooden pail was standing close to it, a rope attached to it and to the hand-cranked roller in the frame above. Crane tested the rope and was not at all surprised when it parted easily. He took his lariat off the horse and with it replaced the well-rope. Then he cast around and picked up a small stone which he dropped into the well and was rewarded with a liquid *plop* when it hit water. Crane lowered the pail.

When he cranked it up, water was streaming from its age-sprung seams, but there would be enough left for his immediate purpose. Crane tasted the water and was relieved to find it both cold and sweet. He took a mouth-spilling drink, then took off his ravaged black hat and tipped the remaining water over his head. Again he lowered the pail and drew it up for the horse.

The next pailful he used to fill his canteen.

Only now, tension draining away from him, was he assailed by a mind-numbing weariness. Slowly, he led the bay to one of the outbuildings and in through the gap where once, double doors had been, and out of the sun's heat. He unsaddled the animal. Then he took his bedroll and the Winchester and trudged across to what had been the main building and went inside.

The several rooms he looked in, apart from scraps of rubbish and rodent droppings, were nearly empty. There was one small table and a couple of broken chairs and several lanterns—all of them dry—but nothing else of interest. All Crane wanted now was sleep. He tossed the bedroll down, shucked his shellbelt, took off his boots and stretched out, tipping his hat over his face. As soon as his eyes closed, Crane was sliding away into a long, deep darkness.

When he began coming back to his

senses, moving stiffened limbs, lifting his head, then stretching painfully, it was with the slow realization that he must have slept not only through what had remained of the day, but through the night as well. That there had been a chill to the night air was now obvious, for he shivered as, moving his cramped limbs, he rolled on to his knees, then stood up. Crane pressed numbed fingers into the small of his back, then, making an effort, picked up his shellbelt and holstered pistol and buckled them on. He took up his hat and put it on.

Outside, the early morning was bright against his eyes, fingers of sunlight reaching across the yard. Water was the next thing. Crane took a quick look around, then crossed to the stone-rimmed well, lowered the pail into it and drew it up again. He had both of his hands around the pail when Jack Geller came easing out of the place where the bay horse was, a pistol in his right fist.

'Jes' stand right there where yuh are,

pilgrim,' Geller said, coming pacing across the yard, spurs clinking, but halted while still some thirty feet from Crane. Geller gave a quick whistle. From behind another outbuilding stepped Reb Stone and Billy Brett—Brett grinning—leading three horses. They came right out into the yard. Reb Stone took charge of all the horses. Billy Brett walked on and stopped twenty feet from Crane and separated from Geller by forty feet. Crane was still holding the pail, water from its fissures running on to the dusty ground and over his boots.

'Never do know what's gonna come walkin' out o' somewheres,' Billy said.

Geller moved his head. 'Bay hoss in yonder.'

Billy nodded slowly, then said to Crane, 'Yuh kin put that down.' Thankfully Crane bent and set the pail on the ground. By the time he straightened up again, Billy Brett had drawn his own rakish pistol and cocked it. Crane felt a sudden tingling sensation in the backs of his knees. This was the moment. Right here and now it could all turn to shit if, on a whim, this grinning pistolman so chose. Brett asked, 'What's your handle mister, an' what yuh doin' in this place?'

'Passin' through,' Crane said.

'Yuh deef, mister? Asked yuh who yuh are.' Brett lifted the pistol higher and tipped his head back slightly, his eyes narrowed.

'Crane ... Abel Crane.'

Billy Brett drew in a long breath entirely through his nose. 'Abel ... Crane ...' He lowered the pistol, letting it hang at his side. 'Abel Crane.' Brett's little black eyes were unwinking. They had been the last thing on earth that some men had seen.

At one of the ruined corrals the skinny, pale-skinned Stone had found a stake still strong enough to hitch the horses, and now came scuffling back into the yard.

Geller said to Brett, 'This feller's mount, it's sure been hard run.'

Brett said, 'That so?' Then, 'So now we

got to wonder what it's drug behind it.'

'Out on the flats, t'other side of them hills, a fat town marshal an' some floursack vigilantes,' Crane said.

'That so?' said Brett again. 'An' still comin'?'

'They're short a few horses,' Crane said. Nobody had made a move to take his pistol from him, but he knew as well as anybody there that it did not matter, for never could he have taken all three, anyway.

The black eyed man asked, 'Yuh know who I am?' When Crane shook his head, said, 'I'm Billy Brett.'

'Well,' Crane said quietly, 'so you're him. Heard about you, Brett.'

That seemed to suit Billy well enough. But suddenly he asked, 'Where's Stoddart?'

Crane's head lifted slightly and Brett looked pleased to have apparently surprised Crane.

After a moment or two, Crane said, 'Word sure does travel.'

Billy Brett nodded slowly. 'Sure 'nough

does. Sure 'nough does. So, where is he?'

'Shook Stoddart,' Crane said. 'Reckon, by this he's down on the Chase River.'

'Or half a day back an' still comin',' Reb Stone suggested.

Crane turned his head to stare at Stone. 'If I thought that, I'd still be headin' south-west.'

'Not fast. Not on that animal in there, yuh wouldn't,' Geller said.

'Chase River,' said Brett. 'Why the hell would Stoddart go there?'

'I was there once before, years back,' Crane said. 'Could be he'd got to hear of it.'

Billy smiled but only with his mouth. 'Never was one to miss a trick ol' Stoddart. Ol' bastard.'

'Well, he missed me,' Crane said, 'but not by much.'

Geller now said, 'Man like Stoddart, he's got to have a real good reason fer stickin' to one man's ass so long.' Evidently, Crane thought, Geller had come to learn a lot about Deputy Marshal Stoddart's hunting of Abel Crane, but now he was probing, testing.

'He thought he had reason enough,' Crane said.

'Such as?' This was the pale man, Reb Stone.

Crane did not at this time know who he was, but simply stared at him. It seemed a long and tensely loaded few seconds. Finally it was Billy Brett who ended it. He gave a short laugh, but his eyes were still cold.

'Yuh're a man likes to take chances, Crane. Yuh sure took one there.' He slid the pistol back in its holster. 'Mebbe we'll git back to that, by an' by.' He drew another long breath. 'Cain't have some maverick on the loose right now, that could fetch the likes o' Stoddart to these parts. An' there ain't jes' me an' these boys here to be considered. Got to keep yuh under my eye fer a time, Crane, like it or lump it. We're gonna take us a spell right here for an hour or two an' then we're gonna head on out.' Geller looked as though he might be about to jump in and have something to say, but Brett gave him a look and Geller chose to keep his mouth shut. 'So,' Billy said, 'yuh ride along with us, Crane, 'till I give yuh the word, one way or t'other. But yuh hear this, mister: one half move I don't like, an' I'll blow your hat through your asshole.'

Four

Some people would hold that the chief problem as far as Edward Stoddart was concerned was that no one could ever be certain where the old bastard was. Tall, gangly, with a stringy neck and bony face, he had grey hair and a thick grey moustache and, at first glance, appeared benign. Yet his eyes were not the eyes of an old man. Like chips of blued steel, they seemed to seize and to hold whatever drew their attention. They were effective, still, over distance, but if the distance was manifestly too great, Stoddart reverted to a brass spyglass. He was using it now while still sitting his black horse, examining a row of bleak-looking soddies along Sour Creek. A few people were standing around down there and, in particular, a big man holding a saddled horse. A visitor, by the looks. Something about the attitude of the man was familiar, but right now the distance defeated even the shuddering disc of the spyglass. So, who he was, Stoddart could not yet tell. In the event, it would be only a matter of time, for what he *could* see was that, whoever he was, he was mounting again and heading in Stoddart's general direction.

So Stoddart simply sat waiting.

A couple of hundred yards closer, the horseman must have become aware of the other man. Maybe looking through a spyglass. The oncoming rider, having been in no hurry, hesitated perhaps thinking matters over, then began advancing again. But Stoddart, patiently fixing him in the glass, saw that the long coat the rider was wearing had been undone and swept back on the right side to expose the handle of a pistol. Stoddart, steadying his own horse, was making no bones about staring through the spyglass until at a certain point he recognized the man coming towards him, on what he saw was a roan horse. He lowered the glass, clicked it shut and, reaching down, restored it to one of his ancient saddle-bags. The other man was coming on steadily, his whole attention on Stoddart. When he was but five yards away he drew the roan to a head-hanging halt and nodded.

'Sure do git about, Ed.'

'Should know well enough, Royce, I go where I'm took.'

Royce Praeger, big solidly built, near as old as Stoddart, with generous white moustaches, once a marshal, sat studying the other man. They went back some way, Stoddart and Praeger, but for some good while their trails had not crossed.

'Picked up word o' yuh,' Praeger said, 'a few weeks back. Some ways from here. Who's this feller I hear you're seekin'?'

Stoddart was scratching slowly at his left shoulder. 'Name o' Crane. Towed me near to five hunnert mile, an' now I lost the bastard, looks like.'

Praeger permitted himself a bleak smile. 'Yuh never was a man to let go, Ed, as I recall.'

Stoddart sniffed and looked idly around as though evaluating the rolling Sour Creek country, the heat-misted rangelands and the low hills westward and, beyond them, the purplish rise of the Holman Range. Closer, the sun caught the wink of strung wire. The telegraph. Near that would be the railroad tracks, for the South-western passed by this place, up a slight incline and between yellow clay cuttings in hills that were clothed in dark pines. Now Stoddart looked again at Praeger.

'Did hear tell yuh was in the horse-tradin' business, Royce.'

Praeger shoved his hat back and scratched at the front of his thick white hair. The hat, Stoddart observed, was brown and well kept, with a silk band and a narrower brim than the hats Praeger had been accustomed to wearing years ago. Maybe it marked a major change in style. Stoddart thought it made Praeger look like a town merchant and that somehow it reduced the intimacy of years ago. As though he was looking at a different man entirely.

Praeger nodded. 'Army contracts here an' there.' He nodded towards the land to the west. 'Outfit down yonderways been runnin' the eye over a few head.' Now, half turning in the saddle, he indicated the soddies. 'Mebbe they seen your man.'

'If they had, they'd likely not say. Crane, he ain't a forgivin' man an' he don't look like one.'

'Cain't say I ever heard tell o' Crane.'

'Your good luck,' Stoddart told him. He rubbed slowly at his wrinkled neck. 'But I've rid as far sou'-west as I'm gonna go. My pick is he's doubled back. Got the notion a while back I was follerin' smoke.' He was telling Praeger only as much as he wanted him to know. Praeger would know well enough the sense to which Stoddart was referring. The feeling that came to some of the old hunters of men, at a certain time, that a trail had gone cold. Something in the mind. Praeger said that, in any case, he had been surprised to come across Stoddart in this region.

Again he said, 'There's been word around. Chase River, some said.'

'Yeah,' Stoddart said, tipping his hat back, dragging a sleeve across his forehead and resettling the hat. 'I did put that notion about, so it might git to Crane's ears. Looks like it's come back to hit a man.'

Praeger nodded. In his view, Stoddart had not changed. Keep 'em guessing. Here and then there. You never could be sure where he might turn up next. But he thought he knew the man well enough to ask, 'Where to now, Ed?'

Stoddart's leathery face creased, but the blue-steel eyes were very still. 'Chase River, mebbe.'

Praeger chuckled. 'An' mebbe not.'

Stoddart shrugged his bony shoulders.

His dirty grey shirt was collarless, but there was a brownish collar stud. His long legs were clad in rough-weave workpants which were almost completely covered by hard-used, studded leather leggings. His boots had seen better days. When Stoddart was out looking for some bastard, appearances counted for nothing. All that mattered was closing in on the quarry. Just get it done. Sometimes Praeger had wondered what might become of Ed Stoddart eventually, what he might have put aside, if anything, from all his years of such work, against the time when he was no longer up to it. And surely that time could not be far off.

To Praeger, Stoddart said now, 'Yuh know me well enough by now, Praeger. Sure don't cotton to lettin' go.'

Praeger said, 'I know it, Ed. I know it.' Then, perhaps to goad a little, 'I do hear tell Sam Yorke's been seen.'

Maybe expecting an outburst, in view of the sad history of Stoddart and Yorke, he was mildly surprised when Stoddart said, 'Heard that, some while back. But I got to say this: what I heard ain't no different from what I heard afore about Sam ever since he went to ground all that time ago. Seen 'im in one place, seen 'im in another. County sheriff up in Saffron claimed to have seen Sam in a saloon there, dealin' faro. Turned out it was some Fancy Dan from Phoenix, Arizona, a good few years older'n Sam an' a good fifty pound heavier.'

Praeger nodded slowly. What Stoddart had said was so, but he said, 'The word that come to me was a whole lot stronger this time.' He was regarding Stoddart from beneath heavy lids. 'Far as I know, the money's still out fer Sam. If'n yuh got a good whiff, I take it yuh'd want to finish it off, fetch that hellhound in?'

'Wantin' an' doin' is two different things,' Stoddart said. 'Five year back, a couple even, yeah, I would. But I got to face it, Royce, ain't gittin' no younger. Comin' out after this Abel

Crane, all this way, that's been bad enough. So, go crawlin' all over the goddamn' country on another rumour o' Sam Yorke?' He shook his head. 'Time, that's what does it. Some o' the fire leaves a man's belly, that's fer sure.' The blued-steel eyes could have belied that.

Praeger was by no means certain, and said, ''Nother name that's come up is Billy Brett.'

'That so?' Stoddart's hard face was unreadable. 'Him an' Sam Yorke was real tight, one time. Mebbe that's where all this here talk o' Sam's comin' from. Somebody seen Billy, so they invented Sam an' all.' Stoddart sat up straight in the saddle, stretching his old muscles. 'Cain't set around jawin' no longer, Royce.' As Praeger came closer they reached out and shook hands, then headed off their separate ways. Praeger north, Stoddart north-east, maybe towards the Chase River country.

They had been riding steadily for some good while across the arid, brushy country, though not pushing the horses, raising clouds of dust, Billy Brett out front by some fifty yards.

Crane, before they left the tumbledown *rancho* had retrieved his rifle while collecting up his bedroll. Certainly there had been no attempt made to have him travel among them unarmed. Which did not mean, of course, that a close eye was not being kept on him. Where Stone and Geller had positioned themselves was not, he felt sure, merely to keep out of the worst of the trailing dust, but to watch him closely as they rode. For Crane was the next rider behind Brett while Reb Stone was some twenty-five yards behind him but a dozen yards out to the left, and Jack Geller a similar distance behind him across to the right.

One thing Crane was glad about was the less-than-urgent pace, for the big bay under him was still sorely in need of a good spell. Crane's worst fear was that because of weariness it might stumble and be incapable of continuing, for he had no doubt that its reward would be a quick bullet from one of these men. They did stop at one point, the event being signalled by Billy Brett's easing down to a halt, allowing the others to come up with him. By that time he was out of the saddle and pissing strongly. They all got down, stretched cramped limbs and took gulps of water from canteens.

Brett nodded in the direction in which they were travelling. 'Starts gittin' green up yonder. But there's a few more mile o' this shit afore that.' Stone said all he wanted was to get shut of this godforsaken place. Geller, sweat running out of the mass of his black hair, said nothing, but continued watching Abel Crane's every move, clearly not happy about Brett's decision to bring the man along.

Brett now said, 'There's a town o' sorts a few mile on. The chow won't be worth lookin' at, but we'll mebbe take a spell anyways.'

Crane was soon to learn that this was typical of Billy Brett, full of purpose one minute, content to kick his heels at the next. Hard to predict what he would do. Men like Billy Brett always unsettled Crane. All now remounted. Not much more than an hour after that, higher country could be seen up ahead, but long before they would reach it they would indeed come into a town of sorts and the bluish haze of smoke now visible foretold of it.

The buildings were all adobe, maybe forty of them, scores of chickens pecking around, and some rough pens, some with pigs in them, a tethered cow here and there, a well, sited in what might be thought of as a market square, a church with a bell-tower and a couple of dingy-looking *cantinas*. One or two mongrels were sniffing around and there was some barking at the new arrivals.

The appearance of the riders at the top end of the dusty main street drew a gathering interest and some apprehension. There could be no mistaking the stripe of the four coming in and now riding abreast.

The visit might have been of no particular consequence but for a simple chance. Chance and Billy Brett's mood at the minute. A little less than halfway along the main street, nearing the town's centre, Billy's eye fell on a girl. Clearly she had been drawing water from the well and was in the act of carrying away an earthenware pitcher, when he arrived and swept his hat off.

'Wa-al now,' said Billy. 'What we got here? Don't yuh go runnin' off! Me, I'm Billy Brett an' I want a word.' And in a lower tone to those who had now drawn rein with him, said, 'An' by Gawd, a word ain't all I want!'

The girl, however, had gone hurrying away, heading in between two adobe buildings, Billy's black eyes following her. There was a tie-rail out front of one of the *cantinas* and Billy led them in towards it. Crane had a feeling that pretty soon it was all going to turn sour, but there was no way he could see that he could avoid becoming involved in what was about to happen.

Five

Stoddart was still on the move but had shifted his direction somewhat. No doubt Praeger, had he observed it, would have concluded at once that such a thing was not unusual and only part of Stoddart's long custom of keeping everybody else guessing.

Indeed, Stoddart had been giving some thought to Royce Praeger. True, they did go back a long way and because of this there had been, to Stoddart's way of thinking, something that had changed about the one-time fellow marshal. It was not simply that Praeger's occupation had changed, that he would have grown away from the old ways, lost the lawman's view. In spite of the easy friendliness, Stoddart had the strange feeling that he had been talking with a total stranger.

There was a small town, Bellich, not much more than a whistle-stop from the railroad, a tiny depot, a water-tower, a mercantile, another place that passed as a hotel, a saloon, a corral and livery, maybe twenty-five houses and some railroad buildings. Cattlemen came here from time to time, but there was not much to come to.

Stoddart himself was not in the town but on a small rise nearby, among a stand of trees, just taking a look, weighing up whether or not to go on down. For there was a telegraph office there. By prior agreement he was due to send a message out from time to time, to the men who had sent him, to report progress. But telegraph offices in small dumps like this always worried Stoddart. Local operators read things and remembered details. Stoddart could not afford to have the wrong word picked up and given wider currency. All tales about this enterprise had to be of his own devising. So he decided against going down into Bellich. But when someone emerged from a livery leading a saddled horse, a sorrel, Stoddart watched as the man mounted and walked the horse on to the main street. Never a man to waste an opportunity, Stoddart took out his spyglass and clicked it open.

Though the angle did not offer a full-face view, what jumped into the disc caused Stoddart to curse softly. He steadied himself, gripping the spyglass firmly, trying to hold the image of the now bobbing horseman, a rider wearing black pants and a black, thigh-length coat and a shallow-crowned, dark-grey hat. The range was long. The man now had his back to Stoddart.

Stoddart lifted his head. Slowly he closed the brass spyglass. No doubt remained in Stoddart's mind; he had been looking at one Jesse Hart. Now, what in the name of God was Hart up to in these parts? A most dangerous man. Stoddart replaced the spyglass in his saddlebag, put a boot in the stirrup and, joints cracking, swung a long leg over the cantle.

The girl had run to where she could find protection. Back to Bascom. At the time, he was lying on a narrow cot in a back room of one of the adobe buildings, having got seriously drunk the day before. Blinking and gasping, he sat up on the cot, his eyes still screwed shut, still dressed in his Levis and pinkish undervest, his face shiny with sweat and prickly with whiskers.

'Aw Jesus! Jesus, Maria ...! A man ain't deef!' It was not easy to follow what had upset her for, as she did when badly upset, she was speaking rapidly in Spanish. Bascom had always had problems with that language. He waved her to silence and demanded that she talk to him in English.

'Men come!'

'Huh? What men?'

Shouting could be heard outside and a hammering on doors. Billy Brett come seeking the big-eyed girl. It would be only a matter of time before the shouting, hammering men arrived at this door. The girl was looking for somewhere to hide. Bascom, the truth dawning on him, suggested she got out another door that gave into an alleyway, but she did not want to get out in the open. Bascom, having dragged his boots on, had now taken up from a table near the cot, an old Navy Colt and fumblingly was checking the loads. He extended a boot towards the cot.

'Git under it an' don't come out.'

The girl gave him a doubtful look, for it seemed like crawling into a trap, but she did as the man directed. The voices outside were getting closer. Bascom cocked the Colt and stepped nearer to the door. There was a window, but today the shutters had not been opened. Somebody began banging on the door and the latch was lifted.

'Hold your peace!' Bascom yelled. They quietened, realizing that, unexpectedly, they were dealing with another *yanqui*. Bascom opened the door. 'What's all the ruckus?' Squinting into the brightness of the day he must have been taken aback by the sight of a round-faced man with fairish whiskers around his mouth and a pair of small black eyes, like rat's eyes, who was standing only four feet from him. There was a taller, heavier man, hat shoved back, exposing a shock of unruly dark hair; another, skinny and older with unnaturally pale skin and a pair of greenish eyes. The fourth man, standing several yards further back, was tall and rawboned to the point of gauntness, spiky black whiskers around his mouth and at the sides of his face. His slate-eyed attention was not so much on the man who had come to the door as the three who were confronting Bascom.

'There was a li'l spic filly, an' she come right along this way. She in there, mister?'

'No she ain't,' Bascom said. He was doing his best to appear confident in the face of this man's disturbing stare. Billy Brett gave a small nod at the Navy Colt.

'Y'allers answer the goddamn' door thataways?'

'Most times,' Bascom said. 'We gits all sorts o' visitors.'

'Jes' so,' said Billy, apparently sympathetic. 'A man can't be too careful. But if I was you, mister, I'd put that thing up now, 'fore it gits to cause yuh a whole lot o' grief.'

'I'll put it up,' Bascom said, 'when this here door's shut an' I kin git some more shuteye.' It was said confidently enough, but the round-faced man was reading what was in Bascom's eyes and coming to a different conclusion. Indeed, Billy's tone changed completely.

'Put it up or not, mister, we're gonna take us a look inside there. Step aside or have that thing took off'n yuh an' shoved up your ass.' Billy had not raised his voice.

When Bascom's eyes flickered, Billy said, 'Four to one. Take me, an' these boys is gonna blow your tongue through your ear anyways.' Brett, though naturally on guard, was not quite prepared for Bascom's move, which was to slam the door and slide the bolt and go spinning away to one side. Hardly had he got out of the way, though, than gunfire erupted and the door was slammed by large-calibre lead.

Bascom said, 'Jesus!' The girl under the cot was whimpering. Bascom told her to shut up, get out and run to the door in the other room and bolt it. There might be four men out there, but they were taking a risk against an armed man, holed up in an adobe building. The shutters in the other room, however, were open, so as soon as the girl had bolted the other door, he called for her to come back into this room. Then he said, 'Git back in where yuh was.' Bascom himself took up a position in an archway between the two rooms. He could watch the unshuttered window and keep an eye on the door that was being shot at. Presently, though, the shooting stopped. Too fly to believe that they had gone away, Bascom resolved simply to stay quiet and let them make the next move.

Outside, Brett, Geller, Stone and Abel Crane had withdrawn, though attention was still on the house where Billy thought the girl was.

Geller muttered, 'Some other bastards back there, Billy.' They looked. Several men had appeared on the main street at a place from which they could see the four strangers. One citizen, at least, had a rifle.

'Cover me,' Billy said.

Stone and Geller drew their pistols and turned to face towards the distant group of townsmen.

Geller said, 'Bunch o' *peons* ain't gonna make no difference, one way or t'other.'

Billy now looked at Crane. 'You an' me, now, mister. Soon see what a bad man's made of. Git on 'round t'other side o' this dump. If that mouthy bastard comes out that way, nail 'im.'

Crane headed away around the adobe house. He had not drawn his pistol. By this time, Jack Geller and Reb Stone had advanced to the main street and the group of men there had backed away a distance of some 150 feet. Geller walked to the hitched horses and fetched his own rifle and Stone's and Billy Brett's. He tossed Stone his, then took Billy's to him.

'Now, that's more like it,' Billy said. He levered a round into the chamber and blasted a shot through window shutters, sending slivers of wood flying. Then he shot at the door and this time when the .44 lead punched it, it shivered under the impact. Billy shot again and whooped when he heard Bascom yelling to hold up. Billy levered the rifle again and waited. He called to Bascom to open up.

There was the sound of Bascom wrestling with the bolt which perhaps had been damaged by Billy's shooting. Before the man inside got the door open the girl's crying and screaming could be heard. She knew well enough what was coming. Bascom was about to throw her to these predators to save his own hide. Bascom was snarling at her to be still even as he was opening the door. As soon as the door came fully open, revealing Bascom, his pistol now put away, Billy, rifle held at the hip, laughed and shot him. Bascom was whacked solidly in the middle of his dirty undervest and knocked backwards, but before he fell he was hit again, this time in the throat. Bascom was flung bodily backwards into a far corner of the shadowed room.

Billy Brett went inside. Crane, on the opposite side of the house, stood still after the shooting ceased, and remained there through the next few minutes, all through the girl's screaming. It sure was loud and must have carried across to the group of townsmen. Finally, Crane walked around the back of the house. Billy was coming out, still settling on his shellbelt. He had a livid scratch down the side of his face.

'Li'l hellcat had to be give a lesson.' *Don't say no to Billy Brett.*

By the time he and Crane and the other two had gathered at the tie-rail it had become clear that more men had come out, these armed with rifles and shotguns. Geller, however, scabbarding his rifle, was dismissive.

'Wouldn't be a pair o' balls among the whole passel on 'em.'

Even as he said it, the Brett party mounting, the group along the street were scattering. Billy laughed. He stopped laughing when it became apparent that the scattering was not to get off the street but to seek cover in doorways and behind crates and casks. As the horsemen hauled away from the rail, several shots cracked, and Stone, turning his horse, made a sudden *huffing* sound and bent forward.

Geller swore and shouted, 'Reb's caught one!'

Geller and Brett drew pistols and began shooting smokily, the horses screwing and stepping beneath them, while Crane came up alongside Stone and put out a hand to steady the swaying man.

Billy was shouting, 'Git Reb away! Git 'im away!'

Crane was doing his best, but the horses were not making it easy for him. Yet somehow he managed to get both his own horse and Stone's under control and then, with one hand bunching Stone's shirt, headed away out of the town.

More shooting came. Crane was aware of the dangerous whipping of bullets. Billy Brett and Jack Geller, now resorting to rifles, were covering the retreat of Crane and the badly wounded Stone.

'Got one!' Billy called in triumph, but he and Geller had to pull out, too, in a hurry, for the townsmen, knowing that they had got a hit on one of the four, were now encouraged to more intensive shooting. It was getting too hot for comfort even for the likes of Billy Brett.

Bart Seligman, his fringe of reddish hair surrounding what resembled a monk's tonsure, was looking somewhat sheepish, so Lola Barrett thought. It was unlike him. So often he tried to be masterful.

'Somethin' wrong, Bart, is there?'

He was restless, walking aimlessly around the room. It seemed he was at a loss to explain what was on his mind. 'Lola, a while back, when I was here, it's possible I could've said something.'

'Said what? I dunno what you mean.'

'Well, at the time,' Seligman said, 'I'd had a few drinks. It's just possible ... I could've mentioned things I shouldn't have.'

'Such as what? I don't remember anything.'

He stopped moving and looked at her directly, perhaps to assure himself that she was perfectly serious. 'Sure about that, Lola?'

'I'm sure. I don't even recall what it was we talked about.'

'Well then ...' Seligman appeared genuinely relieved. She thought he would leave the subject, but he gave her a jolt when he said, 'I did hear that feller Teech had been around.'

Lola looked at him levelly. To deny it, she thought, would be unwise. 'Yeah, as a matter of fact. Passin' through, so he said. I've known him for years. Anyway, you know that.'

'Yeah ... yeah ...' Then, 'You sure he don't mean ... anything to you, Lola?'

'Bart, he's nothin' to me. Now, he'd like to be, I won't deny that. But he ain't. An' he won't be.'

Nodding, he said again, 'Yeah ... yeah ...' Not for a moment did he believe her, but he smiled, still nodding. She was a real fly one, Lola Barrett. But then Seligman was not quite what she took him for, either. He was content that what he had told her, *let slip,* had now passed on.

She moved closer to him and he reached for her.

Six

At one time the place had been a farm. Now it was but the remains of various structures, some of them almost hidden among long grass and weeds and some green brush and a few cottonwoods. They were camped here, two of them.

One was a tall, dour-looking man in maybe his late forties, dirty and unkempt and with a full dark beard and moustaches. He had on a pair of moleskin pants and a dark-red wool shirt with a black leather vest over it. He was wearing no pistol, though a Smith & Wesson Army in a holster, a shellbelt wrapped around it, lay on his bedroll alongside an old Winchester with a very scratched and scored stock.

The other man looked a few years younger, was much heavier-set, muscular, with the shoulders and neck of a brawler. His face was almost clean shaven, his head completely hairless. He had thick lips and a pug nose and very small eyes which glittered out of lardy pouches. Rudy Goss looked what he was, a hard brawler who would as soon rely on his big hands as on the old Walker Colt stuck down the waistband of his pants. Goss had no shirt on, only a filthy pink undervest. The bearded man with him was Sam Yorke.

The sun was not yet high and the night's coolness had scarcely lifted, and from this place, which was on a small rise of ground, the surrounding country in almost every direction, could be observed. Heavy-footed, Goss went to where the horses were picketed among the nearby trees. Yorke took a long look, first to the north, then south, his eyes like stones, his whole attitude, every movement speaking of a growing impatience. He figured that Billy Brett, with others, ought to have shown up by now and that was why he took another long look southwards. Yet from the exact opposite direction would come one man whose message would be the key to what the future held: Bob Teech.

Rudy Goss came out of the trees leading their horses and headed off down a shallow slope towards a brush-clotted stream about forty yards away. Yorke raked broken-nailed fingers through his beard. A disturbing matter, as he had told Jack Geller when he had been here, was the rumour that old Stoddart was on the move. Down this way somewhere. Out after some poor bastard, so it was said. Coincidence. Yorke had always been wary of coincidences. And he had always been much more than wary of Ed Stoddart.

Stoddart reckoned he was about as close as it was prudent to get, having regard to the man he had been trailing. In fact, it had been only during the past couple of hours that he had sought to close up the distance separating them. Stoddart had been taking no chances whatsoever. Now he had left the black tied among some brush and had gone on afoot and laboured to climb in among some slabs of rock overlooking a small *arroyo* some hundred yards further on. He would have preferred to have got in closer, but was not prepared to throw everything away by committing some stupid act at this stage.

The sun was high and its heat, beating down on his back, was like a leaden weight. His knee-joints were troubling him but that was nothing new. It was his lower back that bothered him most and now he had to take care about getting into situations which might require sudden movements. Stoddart faced such things pragmatically and tried not to dwell on them unduly. No longer a young man, what he did have over some others, both old and young, was that his mind was still keen and he could recognize a fool at a good distance and a fake at an even greater one. The man he had chosen to watch was neither.

Stoddart had fetched his spyglass along, but he had taken the precaution of wrapping a bandanna around it to reduce the chances of sun winking off the brass. Grunting, he eased down on his bony elbows, inched along on his belly and settled down to wait. For the man he was interested in had stopped and was making camp, thin smoke rising into the almost windless air. Making camp at this hour could mean any one of several things: the man was spelling his horse in preparation for another, longer leg of his journey; he was here to wait for others; he had become aware that he was being trailed and was now displaying a false normality, designed to deceive a watcher and draw him into a blunder. Stoddart at his comfortable distance, in his uncomfortable posture, settled down to wait. Over the years he had become good at it. He did not put the glass on the man at the camp. He already knew who he was. But if anything else of interest should arise, then Stoddart was ready.

Time went by. An hour had drifted into two, in sweltering heat that was absorbed and given back by smooth rock. From time to time Stoddart had dragged a shirt-sleeved arm across his face, wiping away sweat. But now he lay quite still, squinting into the heat-haze. Beyond the camp, where the fire had been allowed to die, something was on the move. Stoddart focused on it as well as he could, but the sweat was a nuisance. Presently a horse and rider took shape. It was clear that the man at the camp, having walked to the edge of the *arroyo* was watching the approach of the rider. Unalarmed.

Stoddart drew the spyglass to its utmost extent. He had to wait a few minutes before he could get his first clear look. It was the white moustache and then the town merchant's hat that identified the new arrival even before Stoddart could see other details sharply. Royce Praeger. Well, Stoddart thought, *'yuh musta come round in a loop, Royce. Yep, that's what yuh done.'* Coming into the camp, Praeger drew the sorrell to a halt. The man in the knee-length black coat, Jesse Hart, greeted him and took hold of the horse while Praeger stepped down.

It was a meeting that occupied some time, much walking around and nodding and making points and, at one stage, Praeger taking a stick and scratching things on the ground. Hart, hands on knees, studied what had been drawn before Praeger obliterated it with his boots. Finally they shook hands. Praeger remounted and headed away in the direction from which he had come. North, about.

Praeger, seeing Jesse Hart making preparations to leave, concluded that the black-coated man was about to head off in another direction, otherwise he would have gone with Stoddart. Stiff and sore though he was, Stoddart withdrew with a certain haste, not wanting to be discovered should Hart come this way. He went in among brush and stood holding the head of the black horse, stroking it, murmuring to it.

It was just as well that he had moved and got in among some cover, for after only a few minutes he caught sight of Jesse Hart bobbing by only about fifty yards distant, heading south-west. Stoddart stood a while with the horse, thinking about Hart and about Praeger, marvelling that Praeger should have been on such evident good terms with such a man. Ten, fifteen years back, Praeger the marshal would have drawn down on Hart or anybody like him before you could spit. Now Stoddart had to decide if he would do any more about this situation and, if so, which way he would go. But that was only a part of his concerns. The biggest by far, the one that was gnawing at him, was wondering if Abel Crane had succeeded in getting close to Billy Brett and, if he had, Brett had led him to Sam Yorke.

Or if, in the attempt, Crane had met his death.

Sam Yorke, Rudy Goss and Bob Teech had watched them coming in for the past mile and a half, three riders, but it was not until they were within a hundred yards that they realized that one of the three was not Reb Stone. Instead, with Billy Brett and Jack Geller was a long, gaunt, dark-whiskered man, slightly stooped in the saddle, tending to look down. The Brett Party rode into the camp, watched in silence by the three already there.

'Where's Reb?' Sam Yorke said, in a strange, almost forced, husky voice.

'Fell off'n his animal on account o' he was carryin' lead,' Billy said.

'Yuh filled the bastard's boots real fast,' Teech said. All of them were staring at Crane dismounting with Brett and Geller.

'This here's Abel Crane,' Brett said.

Sam Yorke came pacing across to stand in front of Crane. 'So you're the bastard I

93

hear Stoddart's after.'

Crane looked surprised, but said, 'He was. I shook the old hellhound off.'

Yorke knew all about shaking Stoddart off and how difficult it was to accomplish, so he gave Crane an unwinking stare, a look so intense that it seemed he must be trying to penetrate behind Crane's eyes to see into his mind.

'Now tell me, mister, jes' how yuh come to do that.'

All of them had drawn closer, but none of them said anything, not even Billy Brett.

Crane shrugged. 'Ain't sure about that. Figured I'd done it at the Hawk River. I hadn't. What I reckon is, Stoddart's horse threw a shoe. Somewhere around Shannon's Ferry. He dropped way back. No other reason I can think of. I got the break I wanted. Word has it he's down somewhere on the Chase River.'

Yorke thought about it, still staring hard at Crane. 'From where he kin jes' as easy come ridin' back.' Now the bearded man walked away a few paces, obviously weighing in his mind what Crane had said. It was likely that he was thinking that Crane had claimed to have made no fancy moves, claimed no outwitting of Stoddart. Maybe that had been unexpected. When Yorke came pacing back again, he stopped in front of Crane. Yorke's hands were shoved down inside his waistband, his head tipped back slightly.

'What's Ed Stoddart stickin' to yuh like a blowfly in an outhouse *for*, Crane?'

'Crossed a few state lines here an' there,' said Crane. 'The ol' man's got somethin' to prove. They're saying Stoddart's near the end of the line. If he draws a bad card this time ...' Crane made a throat-cutting gesture.

Again, maybe Yorke regarded this answer as unexpected. Genuine. Or clever. He turned his head to look at Brett. 'Where'd yuh come across this feller?'

'Galina Flats. Ol' *rancho* there.' He

nodded towards Crane's bay. 'Near to run out, that'n.'

'How?' Yorke demanded. 'Yuh say yuh'd shook Stoddart.'

Crane spread his hands. 'Run short o' grub. Took a chance an' went into a dump called Arabella. Some gopher-brained town marshal twigged I was the feller Stoddart wanted, an' let fly. I lit out. Next thing there was a posse on my ass. For a bunch o' flour bags they sure did stick at it. In the finish I had to blow a few horses out from under, before the bay dropped dead under *me.*'

'Yuh shot no possemen?'

Crane shook his head. 'Got all set to. Thought about it. Reckoned it'd only set off a whole raft o' telegraphin' here, there an' everywhere. Bring ol' Ed Stoddart back like he was afire, posses all rushin' around.' Again he shook his head.

'Makes sense,' said Billy Brett, who knew a lot about posses.

Yorke drew in a breath and seemed to

relax somewhat. Geller, however, was still not happy; and it was plain that Rudy Goss had taken a dislike to Crane on sight. Yet for the moment at least, attention turned from Crane to Brett. Yorke asked again about Reb Stone.

Billy grinned. 'Jes' plain bad luck, Sam. Passed through some adobe dump I don't even know the name of. Seen a li'l lady there jes' to my taste.' He shrugged. 'Wa-al there was a problem an' words was said an' then it come to pistols an' all. In the finish, some o' them *peons* got theirsel's all worked up an' loosed off some lead. Reb, he happened to catch one. Crane, here, he got Reb on the move, held 'im in the saddle. But five, six mile out o' there, ol' Reb he coughed up some lung and fell clean off'n the horse. So he's out there shovin' up sand.'

If Yorke was angry, and it was likely that he was for there had been no need for this, he kept himself under control. He needed Billy Brett and he needed Geller and Teech and Rudy Goss. And now, he was thinking, he could well need Crane. He did not say this right off, however, but declared that it was time for chow. The group dispersed, some to picket horses, others to get the grub ready.

Yet as Crane was going by, leading the bay, Yorke asked him, 'Heard tell o' Sour Creek?'

Crane nodded. 'Passed through that country once, a good long while back.'

Only when the meal was over and the coffee drunk and quirlies built did Yorke open up. 'Bob's brung us the word, fer sure.' They all looked at Teech. But both Teech and Yorke would know that it would never be accepted without question. For a start, the word of a woman would be looked on with suspicion.

Not unexpectedly then, after Bob Teech had set out the details, it was Billy Brett who said, 'She spins yuh a good yarn. She could spin one to Seligman. They could be settin' us all up.'

This, though probably he would not say so, was something that had been teasing Sam Yorke.

Teech said, 'Seligman, he run off at the mouth.' They thought about that, Seligman and his liking for the bottle. 'It don't make no sense settin' us up,' Teech said.

Billy gave him a look but said nothing. Crane, looking down, his hat shadowing his face, sat listening while bit by bit what was to take place became clear. They were to hit an express car of a South-western freight at a point somewhere along Sour Creek. Though he looked somnolent, Crane's mind was busy. As far as he was concerned there were two possibilities: every man here was entirely unpredictable, dangerously so. The fact that, as a stranger, he had been allowed to listen to this conversation did not mean that he had been accepted as one of them. It could just as easily mean that they were unconcerned because Yorke had already made up his mind that there was no risk, for Crane would not live to tell about it.

If both he and Ed Stoddart had already acknowledged the great risks involved for Crane in this enterprise, then those risks could not be clearer than they were now. To attempt to isolate Sam Yorke and bring him in at last, seemed little more possible now than it had done when it had first formed as a notion in old Ed Stoddart's mind. To employ an unknown, remote bountyman, setting him up as a fugitive and put his name about widely, then get him into the area, not where Sam Yorke was thought to be, but where he was likely to encounter Billy Brett, sooner or later, so went Stoddart's reasoning, where Billy Brett was, eventually Sam Yorke himself would be. Well, against all reason, they had done it. Crane had got in. A man of their own kind.

Now Crane realized that Rudy Goss was watching him. Goss, in a hard voice, said to Yorke, 'That bastard ain't in this.'

The black-bearded man also looked at Crane and said, 'Ain't made up my mind about yuh, mister.'

Billy Brett said, 'Got to decide now, Sam. We ain't got a lot o' time.'

Crane sat very still, looking directly at Yorke. If Yorke was looking for evidence of weakness he was not going to get any. To Crane more than to the others, Yorke said, 'With Reb Stone, there was six. That's about how many I reckon it'll take to git it done, clean. When the freight's stopped, one man to take care o' the horses. One to cover the freight conductor. One up on the loco to take care o' the engineer an' fireman. Three to hit the car, one inside an' two out. Bob reckons it's but a regular freight car, so we use the freight conductor to git inside. There'll be two on guard in there.'

They all thought about it. Finally Billy Brett asked, 'So, what's it to be, Sam?' It seemed that Brett, forever his own man, was prepared to defer to Yorke over this.

'I'll think it over,' Yorke said. He stood up. If there was a fate hanging over Abel Crane it was to stay there for the time being.

Crane wondered where the hell Ed Stoddart might be right now.

Seven

The freight was not yet coupled up. Indeed, the locomotive was not yet on hand. Already standing beneath a lamp on the platform of the Garrick depot, Seligman had become very twitchy. Railroad employees had been despatched hither and yon at his direction, some of them rolling eyes, once out of his sight.

What was to serve as the express car was standing alone at the depot. Other cars and wagons were standing at various places among the lacings of steel in the Garrick yards. Sliding doors were wide open in the car at the depot. Often a bustling place, now that evening had come down there was little activity, the yards a shadowy wilderness.

Seligman was always nervous when

organizing anything, the more so on this occasion, knowing that the die was all but cast and that soon, Praeger, overseeing Wells, Fargo men, would fetch a wagon around to the depot. This would bring personal baggage, his and Praeger's, and also thirty-six small canvas sacks bulging with currency. Now, having for the moment retreated into an unlit office at the depot, he reached a silver flask from an inside pocket of his coat and took a long, gasping draught. To settle his nerves. He was hoping to God that he would be able to hold himself together, all through, and not expose weakness to the narrow-eyed Praeger, a man who seemed always unfazed no matter what the circumstances. Ex-marshal. Horse-trader. God knew what else. A hard man to read, Praeger, but one who, within himself, carried some old resentments. Seligman was quite sure of that. He put the flask back in the inside pocket. It was a comfort to know that in one of his bags there was an unopened quart bottle.

Seligman walked back out on to the ill-lit platform. A young, fresh-faced deputy came. When there was a rattling sound at the other side of the depot, Seligman turned to watch the central doorway. Quite soon the Wells, Fargo, agent, Purkiss, a man with a round, flushed face and wearing a grey derby hat, came through, leading a succession of others wheeling trolleys loaded with Seligman's and Praeger's personal baggage. Clearly these men were not travelling light, and Seligman, by way of explanation said that they intended *stopping over a while* once the delivery had been safely made. At Seligman's orders the baggage was loaded into the express car.

Now the white canvas sacks had begun arriving on other trolleys. Praeger walked in right behind them. He was carrying a Winchester. Somewhat ostentatiously, Seligman held up a hand bringing the small procession to a halt. He stepped into the open express car, then personally set about loading the canvas sacks, counting them as he did so.

'Thirty-six,' said Seligman finally. The Wells, Fargo agent came to Seligman with a paper clipped on a board. From a pocket, Seligman took a stub of pencil and signed for the consignment. Praeger came and stood just outside the door. The deputy now approached carrying a two-barrelled shotgun and tried to hand it to Seligman. Seligman, however, waved it away. 'Never did cotton to them things. There's a rifle in here, an' there's this.' He opened his coat to disclose the handle of a Colt Lightning, the weapon holstered high on the hip on the left side.

The railroad and Wells, Fargo man left. The freight conductor arrived. The deputy stayed. A locomotive was on the move, blowing rushes of smoke into the night sky, and it began working up and down the yards, building the train. A caboose was coupled on behind the express car. Three freight cars, already loaded elsewhere, were coupled together ahead of the express car. Neither Praeger nor Seligman watched this operation. Both were inside their car testing the locks on doors at either end and those which would secure the sliding doors at the side. Seligman was sweating profusely.

'Git a-hold,' Praeger said.

Seligman produced his flask and took a swig. He knew better than to offer one to Praeger.

What started it Crane would have been hard put to say, but it did seem that it had been inevitable. Maybe Yorke had said something, or Billy, or maybe it was all down to Rudy Goss himself. Whatever the reason, Crane felt in no great shape to handle it. One way and another he had been pushed close to his limits. A brief exchange of sharp words, Goss's dislike on sight of the gaunt man who had come riding in with Billy Brett. There had arisen a quick, ragged scuffle in passing, Goss sour, evil-tempered, Crane knowing that, whatever happened, he must not back down. To do so, to show weakness, would mean an instant loss of any standing he had gained among these unforgiving men.

Crane's hat had gone spinning away and he had staggered back before steadying and facing the bald, muscular man who had discarded the pistol that he had been carrying in his waistband. There was immediate interest. Sam Yorke and Billy Brett standing some forty feet away, having earlier been in low-voiced discussion, merely looked on, almost casually, without expression. Jack Geller and Bob Teech, who had been over near the horses, now came wandering closer, Geller grinning, most likely at the prospect of Abel Crane being handed a beating, for in Geller's mind, tangling with Rudy Goss would surely make that a foregone conclusion. There was no comment from

Yorke himself now, about the number of men he thought would be needed at Sour Creek, something that seemed to have been much in his mind earlier. He might be about to lose one of his six.

It was obvious to Crane what he was up against. Rudy Goss, though not quite as tall as Crane, was thick-necked and muscular, and his attitude proclaimed strength, brutality and a confidence born of his violent history. They were moving among long grass and weeds. Crane was concerned that if he should stumble and fall, then it might well be over before it had properly begun. Yet he had to keep on the move to try to avoid Goss's heavy, swinging punches, for there were to be no tentative, cautious prods by Goss. He came in strongly at Crane, who had to retreat watchfully. The other men looked on. No one spoke. No one called out. Goss came lumbering after Crane, ham-like forearms raised, huge fists clenched, wanting to smash the other man to the ground, then send the boots pounding in. If that should happen, if Crane should go down, within reach of those boots, he knew that Goss would never let up until he had crippled his victim.

Crane, forearms held up defensively, managed to block one arching punch, but was still jolted by it and sent staggering sideways. Yet in his eagerness to get to grips with Crane, for an instant Goss left himself open and Crane, summoning all the energy he could, jumped in and drove his left fist at Goss, catching him full in the left eye, the impact whacking the brawler's head back as though it had been hit with a wheelspoke. Crane was not quite fast enough, however, to follow up with a right hand, for Goss, although hurt by the blow, was fighter enough to go twisting away, throwing up a blocking arm as he did so. At the last moment Crane held back the second punch. Just as well, for Goss, unused to taking retaliation, came storming back. A cut under the left eye had sprouted bright blood, and already thick bruising was coming up, threatening to obscure his vision.

But now Goss knew that rushing the quicker man could leave himself open, so began following Crane tenaciously but more guardedly. And by so doing became more dangerous than ever. He would take his time, get properly positioned before landing one of his killer blows. Sooner or later he must pick Crane off. Goss must have realized that Crane was in no great shape and must soon be worn down.

From that point on, Crane began to feel the heavy jolting of Goss's blows, for some of them were beginning to find a mark. Though so far managing to protect his head he was beginning to take heavy punishment on his body and his arms. And twice Goss had lashed out with a boot, trying for one of Crane's knees, but both times the gaunt man had retreated in time. Goss's left eye had now all but closed, the flesh around it grossly swollen and Crane took advantage of that to move as often as he could to Goss's left so that the man was compelled to keep turning in order to see Crane clearly out of his good eye. Both fighters were grunting and gasping, the noises seeming loud, for the men looking on were still doing so in a silence that was almost uncanny. Only one of the horses stirred occasionally.

Goss swung a looping left and this time Crane was not quick enough, the blow catching him on the side of the head. He hit the grassy ground rolling and, though half stunned, instinctively went crawling away for, as he had expected, Goss came pounding in to follow up the advantage. Even as Crane dived away, a boot caught him a glancing blow on the thigh. Crane went over on his back and lashed out with both boots. There was solid contact as the oncoming Goss took the impact in his midriff, a burst of breath coming from him. Crane, breathing harshly, now unclasped his shellbelt and tore free the holster-thong, and when he came lurching to his feet, was relieved of that encumbrance.

Goss was now several feet away, hands clutched at his solar plexus, body arched forward. Crane went in and hit him in the face, feeling the sharp pain of the blow in his own hand and up his arm. But solid though the punch was, Goss staggering from the shock of it, the brawler did not go down. Crane, looking for another chance, wondered how hard he would need to hit this man in order to put him down. Crane himself was having to draw in great gulps of air. His arms and legs were aching, his hands pulsating with fiery pain. He could not continue this for much longer, and even as he tried to get in another punch, Goss was recovering, blocking it, swatting one of his own at Crane, the big fist skidding off Crane's shoulder. Goss was now so close that his breath was hot in Crane's face and Goss suddenly grabbed Crane around the middle.

At this, the strength of the man became more obvious than ever, for Crane found himself in a grip so firm that breath was driven out of him. But his arms had not been pinned. Goss's shiny head was pressed into Crane's chest and even as Crane felt himself being swung savagely right and left, as though in the grip of a bear, he brought one of his elbows hard down on to the crown of Goss's head. The result was that for a second or two the fierce grip slackened. Crane struck again with the hard point of the elbow and, with a huge effort, went twisting away. Once free, he struck hard at Goss's face and connected again. They separated.

Both fighters were bleeding, Goss even more so than Crane. Yet Crane had about reached the end of his strength, hardly able to raise his arms to defend himself, much less launch another attack. Goss, shaking his head and letting out a roar of fury, came right at Crane who braced himself. But a piece of luck intervened, for Goss, slowed by Crane's unexpectedly strong defence, blood now getting in his good eye, stumbled in the bunch-grass. Crane closed with the man and, as Goss's head lowered, brought a knee up, and this time had the satisfaction of feeling the solidest of hits, Goss's head being jolted upwards, blood spraying from it. Crane gathered himself for one final effort and, seizing Goss by the back of his thick neck, jerking his head down, brought the knee up a second time, smashing it into Goss's face. The big man, flung backwards, sat down hard, then fell over sideways in the weedy grass. By that time Crane himself was on hands and knees, his head hanging, his mouth and nose dripping blood and mucus, a roaring noise in his ears, his many abrasions feeling like separate fires, his chest heaving, his lungs desperate for air.

Only now did the other men come forward, and it became clear that Sam Yorke's only concern was that, whether or not what had taken place had been some kind of testing of Abel Crane, he was now reduced to four fit and able men. Yet when Crane began coming to a clearer awareness, it was to find that they were regarding him (even Jack Geller) in a new way. No one there could recall when another man had come even close to beating Rudy Goss. The fact that this unprepossessing newcomer who had looked to be in poor shape to begin with, had managed to do it, seemed reason for some degree of respect. But if anybody else had chosen to launch a blow at him, Crane would likely have fallen over before it landed. He was utterly spent. After a while he did manage to get on his feet and went blundering across to where he had shucked the belt, holster and pistol.

Jack Geller walked to the fallen Goss and prodded him with a boot.

To Crane, Yorke said, 'Git on down to the crick. Git yourself fit to fork a horse.' Obviously, no concessions were to be made.

Uncertainly, Crane went down the shallow slope, pushed through green brush, lay down and scooped cold water over his head, gasping from the shock of it. He lay there for a time trying to shut out of his mind, pain and stiffness and the fire in his throat and chest. Vaguely he could hear voices and the getting ready of horses, the animals blowing, bit-chains clinking. He did not know if he would be able to get up again.

Eight

The South-western freight was rolling, smoke tumbling out of the big stack, down along the length of the train, washing into the night sky behind it. They had lit a lantern inside the express car and by its yellowish glow, old Praeger was looking older than ever, and Seligman, taking regular pulls from his silver flask, was paler and more red-eyed than ever. He had a film of sweat on his skin.

The freight conductor, a small, sandy-haired individual, was back in his caboose, no doubt with his stove going, enjoying some comfort, and he had not yet availed himself of the arrangement he had insisted on, rapping on the door to be allowed to pass through to his freight cars. ('Stuff can get spilled or leak. My responsibility.

119

Rules say I gotta check.') Officiousness, more like. Seligman would have preferred to have had the express car coupled on last, but had been advised that this was not an acceptable position.

Royce Praeger was sitting on a fold-down canvas seat. His townified hat set aside, he was smoking a fat cigar and doing his best not to lose patience with his undeniably jumpy companion. The liquor the man had been drinking (having replenished the flask from a bottle taken from his baggage) so far had done nothing to dampen his nervousness. Praeger thought that before too much longer he was going to have to speak to Seligman.

In the end, however, their joint purpose must prevail and Praeger could not afford to risk a serious rift. Broodingly, while affecting to doze lightly while enjoying his cigar, the once-marshal was keeping a close eye on Seligman.

Now Seligman was saying, 'Be glad when it's done with, Royce, by God I will!' Praeger, in his cloud of cigar smoke, did not respond, apparently occupied with his own thoughts, but Seligman was concerned that the man was by no means as somnolent as he seemed to be. Seligman was sure he was being scrutinized. It made him doubly uncomfortable. Uppity old bastard, Praeger. Seligman was convinced he was being found wanting by the white-moustached man. It gnawed at him. There were other things, too, that were troubling Seligman, and not only the realization that he had set in motion events which, if he had been able, he might have reversed. Lola Barrett. He took another swig from his flask. The depths of human deceits were unfathomable. In other circumstances, the car, rocking under him, might have lulled him into sleep, but would not do so now. Seligman was being borne onwards towards something known, yet not wholly known. With icy fingers it clawed at his belly.

Every inch of Crane's body seemed to be

achingly afire. Sweating, unshaven, stoop-shouldered in the saddle, he was trying to shut the pain from his mind, but not succeeding. The camp, such as it had been, was behind them and they were riding out across undulating country, the ultimate goal, Sour Creek. But that was some way off. And the way things had shaped up, Crane had become trapped in this enterprise

If Crane looked and felt bad, so did Rudy Goss. The husky man's left eye was now completely closed and it was almost sure that his nose had been broken. Certainly, the fight with Crane had left him hang-headed and silent. Yet every time a glance out of his undamaged eye fell on the gaunt rider, it carried a message of pure malevolence. Incomprehensibly, Crane had beaten him. This time. Goss was by no means a man who would simply accept such a humiliation.

What they had seen had had an effect on the others, too. Jack Geller, riding alongside Billy Brett, behind Sam Yorke and ahead of Crane, had not turned his head once since they set out, but Crane was in no doubt as to that man's dislike of him. It seemed to come off Geller like the stench of his body. Riding at the back of the party, Bob Teech had been watching both Goss and Abel Crane. Teech would have put his roll on Goss beating the other man to a pulp. Men who had been in far better shape than Crane had been thrashed into bloodied rags by the big man. So Crane had either been the luckiest goddamn' pilgrim in Creation or there was a whole lot more to the bastard than met the eye. Teech's attention shifted further ahead, beyond all the others, to Sam Yorke. The black-bearded man was out front there with his own thoughts, and best left to them, so Teech believed. And what Yorke really made of this Abel Crane was by no means clear. Maybe something, somewhere, did not smell quite right.

Crane, though hurt and not relishing

this time in the saddle, now had to face the truth. The bold plan to somehow isolate Sam Yorke and get him to where Crane hoped that Stoddart would be, had been thin enough to begin with. Now it seemed to be beyond possibility. There was, too, a hint of fatalism in the persistent thought that, unlikely as the plan had been, it had gone well in the early stages, Stoddart assiduously sowing the seed of the notoriety of a man named Abel Crane and the success in getting close to the dangerous Billy Brett. Crane had taken a terrible chance and it had come off. So far. For in spite of his getting the better of Rudy Goss, he could almost feel the gnawing suspicion that some, perhaps all, in this party, had of him. Stoddart came into his mind again. *Ed, I sure do need some help.* Crane thought that, in the foreseeable future, there was small chance of that being forthcoming.

Late in the day, his own long shadow

and the sorrel's cast before him, Jesse Hart came weaving in and out between brush near a long, gentle incline where the telegraph wire was strung and railroad tracks gleamed. The black-coated man had not entered the town of Morland, which was the nearest community to this place, having no wish to arouse undue curiosity. Going into the other place, Bellich, in daylight, might not have been wise either, so he now thought; for ever since, he had been prey to an uneasy feeling that unseen eyes had been fixed on him. Because of it he had been prompted to alter direction abruptly from time to time, even dismounting among covering brush, or in some *arroyo*, waiting to find out if a rider might put in an appearance. There had been nothing, only the endless silence of this remote place. No rise of birds that might have given away another presence.

Even so, walking the horse through the dying day, he now brought it to a halt once again, then made a complete turn to look back the way he had come. It so happened that at this hour there was little wind, so any rise of dust must surely be made by a horseman. Hart stared back, then left, then right. He pulled the sorrel around again and continued on his way. Though he was hungry he decided against making a camp. It was better to light no fire.

A good half-mile away, Stoddart, the black horse tied to brush, saw the small figure that was Jesse Hart come to a stop and turn around and remain motionless for a few minutes before moving on. Stoddart was not using the glass. Old dog. Up sun. He knew who Hart was and where he was. The man had been changing his line of ride from time to time. Suspicious. Stoddart had expected that. Now he was interested in whether or not Hart would make a camp. Yet as time went on he showed no inclination to do so. It puzzled Stoddart somewhat. Hart was not a man inclined to spend time in places such as this, merely riding around. Towns had more appeal. Yet he had not gone into Morland when he had had the chance. True, it was a dingy, dirty dump, nothing to recommend it to a sober man, but Hart could have got a meal there and a few drinks, had he been so inclined. Stoddart rubbed a coarse hand over whitish stubble and thought about Hart. And Royce Praeger. Strange currents were running. And he thought about Abel Crane. God help him.

Rudy Goss's horse had gone lame. There was nothing else for it, they would have to stop. Sam Yorke was cussing fit to fry the animal. Goss got down.

Yorke said, 'Git the kak off him.'

Goss, moving poorly, loosed the cinches, then dragged off the saddle, blanket and bedroll. Presently the lame horse stood bereft of all gear, and Sam Yorke came forward and shot it where it was. The horse fell, kicking, then lay still, a small amount of dust rising.

Billy Brett said, 'Double-mounted, Rudy's gonna make the next'n go lame.' That seemed highly likely. And in view of what was to come, they could not afford to have another horse shot. Yorke expelled a long breath. Crane thought about it, wondering if they might simply take his horse and leave him here afoot. Or dead. But Billy said to Yorke, 'I recall there's a small spread not far off, thataways.' They all looked the way he was indicating.

Yorke nodded and said, 'You go, Billy. You, Bob. Take Crane along. Latch on to a good saddler. Don't give a shit how yuh do it, jes' git it done.'

Billy Brett took these instructions with what Crane thought was surprising calm, and nodded easily to Teech and to Crane. 'Let's go.' He took the bridle that had been on Goss's horse and they all three headed away across the rolling country, leaving Sam Yorke, Jack Geller and Rudy Goss with the dead horse. Why he had been chosen to be one of the riders Crane had no idea, unless it was to be one further test. Following Billy Brett, he rode alongside Bob Teech, a man not inclined to make conversation. Yet it had been Teech, so Crane had gathered, who had come by the details of the express car shipment on the South-western, and this through a woman whose name was Lola Barrett. It had meant nothing to Crane, nor had the name Seligman. Indeed, the entire South-western enterprise that Sam Yorke was about to engage in had come unexpectedly into the picture, a complication of large proportions, yet of which even Stoddart must have heard no whisper.

They rode for an hour across what plainly was rangeland, encountering a few white-faced cattle but no other riders. Half an hour later, coming around some high brush, Billy Brett held up a gloved hand and all three came to a halt. Before them, some hundred yards away, stood ranch buildings and a corral. There seemed to be little activity. In the corral could be seen several cow-ponies and a few saddlers.

'Cain't go pussyfootin' around,' Brett said. 'Got to git in an' take what's wanted.' He turned a grinning face towards Crane. 'An' you're elected.' Billy slid his Winchester from its scabbard. Teech did likewise. 'We'll come in another forty, fifty yards an' we'll cover yuh.' He gave the bridle and reins to Crane.

To have refused or even to have seemed reluctant would have invited instant retribution. Crane did not so much as bat an eye. He nodded, riding forward with them until, at about fifty yards out, Billy Brett and Bob Teech stopped and Crane went on alone, holding the bay to a walk.

Approaching the ranch buildings—a large, low-roofed ranchhouse, several out-buildings, a bunkhouse, cookhouse and a barn, all set around a hardpack yard—Crane angled in so that, as far as was possible, he would be screened by the barn, while heading directly to the pole corral.

Still there was no evidence of habitation. No challenge. When reaching the corral he dismounted and light-hitched the bay to it, he then unslipped his lariat and moved around the corral to where a rope-hinged section gave access. But now he was in the yard itself. Crane ducked his head and stepped through into the corral, disturbing some of the horses, setting them on the move. It might well draw some interest, but he was too far committed to bother about that now.

Running his eye over the few saddlers here, he judged the best of a poor lot to be a roan, and this was one of the horses now on the move. Crane shook out the loop of his lariat and began closing on the horse, but it tossed its head, blowing, and went ambling away from him. Crane followed. He was sweating and still moving stiffly, far from recovered from his hard encounter with Rudy Goss. The irony of his being here now, trying to steal a mount for that same man, would come to him later. A cow-pony passed across his path, then there was the roan. Out went the stiff loop, dropping over the horse's head. Crane tightened the loop, then hastened forward. He settled the horse. There was no more resistance. The lariat removed, he slipped the bridle on, settling the bit. He coiled his lariat, then led the roan to where he could take it out into the yard. He was content to leave the corral open. If other horses took the opportunity to come out, whoever was around here might have their work cut out rounding them up.

Somebody *was* around. From the direction of the cookhouse came a reedy-voiced yell. A man in a grubby white apron appeared in the doorway and, almost at the same time, someone came out of the ranchhouse. Then a couple of men from the bunkhouse. Crane was on the run now, heading around the corral, the roan going with him. A pistol was fired, but there was no sense of lead coming anywhere near Crane. Maybe the shooter had been afraid of hitting the roan. Crane ran on around the corral, desperate to get to where his own horse was, get mounted and get out of here. The bare-faced effrontery of this theft of a horse in broad daylight from a place such as this, was likely to set a swarm of pursuers out after the thief, baying for his blood. If he was caught he would be lynched. That was the way things were. But Billy Brett and Bob Teech might well get away. *'Too bad about Crane.'*

Now there was a whole lot more shouting. There came a lashing shot from a rifle. If Brett and Teech had not been noticed before they sure would be now. Billy in fact gave a whoop, and even from a restlessly moving horse, aimed his rifle and cracked a shot away, laughing. Teech had his eye on Crane, now mounted and engaged in getting the roan horse to follow. Somebody at the ranch had got hold of a rifle. Crane heard it go off as he began working his way towards Brett and Teech and his blood was chilled by the sound. But now both Brett and Teech were shooting, levering and shooting again, the ejected, spent shells glittering.

Billy was yelling out to Crane, 'C'mon fer Chrissake!'

Crane was doing his best, the roan seeming not quite as willing now. He went bobbing on by Brett and Teech without even a glance, while they, on turning, skitter-stepping mounts, continued shooting. Then they began a gradual retreat. Crane's hope that the other corral horses might come out had been rewarded. There was a lot of hat-waving and rounding-up going on.

Now Crane and the stolen horse were joined by the other two riders. Billy was highly amused, apparently unconcerned at the probability of pursuit. Teech was looking more thoughtful and looking over his shoulder.

'Nailed one o' them cow nurses,' said Billy. 'Sat the bastard down on his ass. Two-bit outfit.' The brand on the roan would subsequently reveal the ranch to be Diamond L.

Crane did not like the sound of a ranch-hand being shot. They rode on, Billy Brett urging Crane to greater speed.

Teech, still looking, said, 'Nobody comin' yet.'

They were passing in among brush, Brett and Teech still tending to hang back, allowing Crane to go on ahead, which was some comfort, since obviously they were intent on persuading any following riders to think twice about getting too close. But there was no further shooting. After they had put another couple of miles behind them, the other two ranged up once more alongside Crane, rifles scabbarded, apparently satisfied that they were in the clear and would stay that way.

Crane had a hollow feeling in his stomach. He had ridden with Billy Brett. He was now a horse thief. And back behind them a man had been shot and, for all they knew, fatally shot. Come seeking Sam

Yorke, he had become part of an existence which put no value whatsoever on human life. And there would be more of this to come.

In the run-down town of Morland, Lola Barrett was once again engaged in packing. *Pack to leave. Unpack when you get there. Pack again to leave.* Her life seemed to have become an endless succession of packings and unpackings. She could but hope—believe—that it would all turn out to be worth it. The thing you could never be certain of was trust. No matter how much care was taken, in the end, in something like this anyway, you had to finish up trusting somebody to do what they said they would do.

Lola glanced around the room and had to suppress a shudder. It was dirty, in a dirty little hotel on a dirty street, in a town from which the very spark of life seemed to have died long ago. She thought that if she had had to stay in this place a day longer, she would have gone mad. Sighing, she folded a garment and pressed it down inside an open leather bag on the bed. Her visitor had come and gone a little while back, in the night. The last contact. He had been confident that he had come in and would go out with nobody the wiser. She had waited all day for him and had begun to think that he was not coming. They had not had many meetings, just enough. Now she had a growing feeling that was half excitement, half apprehension. There could be no turning back now. She had to play her final part and then it would be goodbye to all dumps like this one.

She came to the last item to be dealt with. She did so with a sense of distaste. Fear, even. In the top drawer of the battered bureau lay an old pistol. It was an 1876 Merwin and Hulbert .44 calibre, six-shot, single-action weapon. In all, twelve inches long, it weighed about two pounds ten ounces. This one had a hardwood handle and had been given to her, as she recalled, by Bob Teech who, long ago, had even instructed her in the firing of it. (*'Never do know when it could make the difference.'*) And, surprisingly, because she had long-fingered hands, she had been able to manage the thing. But she had never liked having it among her possessions. She had never thought it wise to keep it. Until now.

Nine

Obviously Sam Yorke had given much thought to where along Sour Creek the South-western was to be hit. He had led them there with every evidence of confidence. At this particular spot, the rails were laid through a stretch of rough terrain, brush and smooth boulders on either hand. Thus the men who would await the approach of the train would be afforded cover and the means to bring the freight to a stop. The chosen place was some good way from the scattering of soddies to be found along Sour Creek.

From time to time Crane had taken a long look out across the country to the north-west. If any riders should be out and searching for them, men from the Diamond L outfit, it would not be easy to see them approaching until they were uncomfortably close. Yet as time went on it seemed less likely that any would come. If the possibility had occurred to Billy Brett he had given no signs of concern. It was only an hour or so to sundown.

Now, of Bob Teech, Billy asked, 'What time's that freight pullin' out?'

'Tonight,' Teech said. 'Late. This time tomorrer we'll be away free an' clear.' There was to be more to that than Crane knew.

The black-bearded Yorke had heard them. 'It will, if'n y'all do like I say to do.' His attention swivelled to the quiet, battered Rudy Goss. 'Remember, soon as it's stopped, git on up on that loco real sharp. Make goddamn' sure the engineer an' the fireman don't go nowhere nor touch nothin'. Once it's stopped it stays stopped.' Now he stared at Crane. 'Same time as Rudy's puttin' the word on that crew, climb on the caboose an' stick a barrel in the freight-conductor's ear. Walk the bastard to the express car. It's his voice they got to hear. They open up, let him in or yuh blow one in his ear.'

Yorke's plan was a simple and brutal one: simple to the extent that all should go well if all parties did exactly as they were told; brutal in that no time would be wasted with those who did not.

So Crane was to be given the task of getting inside the caboose to put a pistol on the freight-conductor. That man must then be taken along to persuade those in the express car to open up. A refusal meant that the freight-conductor was to be shot. In that event, Yorke, Geller and Teech would commence punching holes in the car with rifle bullets. Yorke had reasoned, 'They want to discard their hands on account o' some other bastard's money, that's their business.' Simplicity once again. Crane tried not to dwell on what might happen if the freight-conductor proved to be the kind of fool who tried to resist a bandit holding a pistol.

Crane was still in bad shape. The ride to and from the Diamond L had not helped. As soon as their very frugal meal was over he crawled under his blanket, head resting on his saddle. The sole comfort, otherwise, was that Rudy Goss was still moving around as though having trouble with his vision. The horses picketed some fifty feet away, one by one the rest of the party settled down to sleep.

Though his eyes were closed, Crane's mind was busy. The possibility that he would get a chance to take Sam Yorke was, he now believed, all but non-existent. An ambitious, perhaps foolhardy notion in the first place, his present physical shape and the unexpectedness of this enterprise stood against his ever being able to get close to Yorke while the man was on his own, let alone put a pistol on him. *Too bad, Ed.* To get out of this with a whole skin, without having to injure some innocent party, or worse, kill somebody, was all he could hope for. And there were still strong currents of suspicion running here, even after Stoddart's theatre of the chase, even after the stealing of the horse. If that, indeed had been a test, then he had come through it. Yet Jack Geller, for one, still watched him sourly, and Bob Teech. Teech had never been content with Billy Brett riding blithely in with Crane in tow.

If Abel Crane was apprehensive of his immediate future, Seligman was in no better shape, if for different reasons entirely. Sitting on one of his own items of baggage in the noisy, rocking express car, he had made considerable inroads into his supply of whiskey. Opposite, sitting with his arms folded and his head sunk down on his chest, Praeger could well be asleep. Or maybe he was feigning sleep, merely wishing to avoid further conversation with Seligman. But Seligman, his mind now host to all manner of demons, needed above all to talk, needed to hear reassurances, needed

... what? Strength? Yes, some of old Royce Praeger's solid strength.

Seligman all but dropped his flask when there came three solid knocks on an end door of the car. He started to his feet and almost lost his balance. Praeger's head jerked up.

'What?' So maybe he had been asleep.

From the other side of the door the freight-conductor's voice called, 'Cawfee!'

It was Praeger who got up and went over, a mite unsteadily because of the motion of the car, and unbolted the door. The round-faced, fresh-complexioned railroad man, carrying steaming mugs, nodded and grinned and came on in. Quite steady on his feet. Practised.

Almost furtively, Seligman put his flask away and grasped one of the coffee mugs with both hands. Praeger took his and also took a silver watch from a vest pocket and thumbed it open.

'How long to Morland?'

''Bout an hour.'

'We stop there,' Seligman put in, his speech slightly slurred.

'Yep,' the freight-conductor said. 'Take on water at Morland. An' some freight. Not much. Stopover mebbe twenty minutes.' It would be daylight by then.

'In that dump,' said Seligman, 'it wouldn't want to be longer.'

The freight-conductor headed on back to his caboose with its stove, and Praeger bolted the door behind him. Seligman blinked fluid eyes at Praeger and said nothing. He did not have to. Morland. Well, they were on the way and no mistake. It was impossible to know what Praeger was thinking. Except that he probably thought less of Seligman than he had done at any other time.

Stoddart though he had slept soundly through the night, through sheer need of rest, was still doing his best to keep Jesse Hart under some sort of scrutiny. It had not been easy, without getting too close to the man. Stoddart figured that he would be hard put to it to match Hart, now, if it came to that. Yet Stoddart had not been able to answer the nagging question about why he should be allowing this man to distract him from his main purpose, which was to lend some support to Crane if that were to be at all possible. The teasing notion, however, was that Jesse Hart's very presence down here, and his meeting with none other than Royce Praeger, meant that something highly unusual was going on. It seemed to Stoddart that this was maybe some kind of link in a chain of unusual events, things drifting around on the wind. Billy Brett on the move, coming north. Sam Yorke said to be back. The link between Brett and Yorke was easy to accept. Where Jesse Hart might possibly fit was less simple. And somewhere in the middle, if indeed he was still alive, was Abel Crane. Crane had needed money real bad. A man would have to need money real bad to get into this. Stoddart now wondered—having for long enough suppressed the thought—if he, as the broker in the deal, in his own anxiety to nail Yorke, had acted without a shred of conscience. Facing it now made him distinctly uncomfortable. It was a state of mind he had not expected to have to endure.

Stoddart's old head lifted. He led the black horse away from the paltry creek where it had been slaking its thirst and up in among some high brush, where he stood at its head, murmuring to it, rubbing its warm nose. His ear had caught a sound and, though it had not been close by, it had been sufficient to compel him to act cautiously and seek cover. He did not think that it was Hart, doubling back. It had not been that kind of sound.

Stoddart reached to an arm of brush and pulled it down to get a view. And there it was, some 300 yards away, a small covered wagon with a four-horse team, glimpsed between clumps of brush, moving slowly, perhaps coming to a stop down there at the creek. He could not get a clear view of the driver. There had appeared to be but one figure on the wagon-seat. Stoddart thought it best to take no chances and stay out of sight. True, it might be only some ranch wagon, or some itinerant merchant, lately in Morland, but the fewer people who knew of his presence, the better.

Patiently, Stoddart waited a good hour. He had heard the wagon on the move again after a pause of no more than ten minutes, but because it was headed in the same direction that he was, he wanted to let it get well clear before he emerged and attempted to resume his tracking of Jesse Hart. He realized that at some time he might well sight the wagon again, but it would be ahead of him and therefore avoidable. Hart had seemed to be in no great hurry, so Stoddart believed that he would soon come up with the man again. Away across to the left, in an easterly direction, was the telegraph wire and the railroad tracks. It was almost as though Jesse Hart had been keeping in touch with them. Idly, Stoddart wondered when he might sight a train. So far there had not been any, headed in either direction.

Ten

It was not until Sam Yorke drew all of them together at the Sour Creek campsite that Crane realized that eventually he would have to part with the bay horse. They had been about to pick out a couple of boulders small enough to be manhandled on to the track, but big enough to cause the engineer to bring the freight to a stop.

The place chosen was around a shallow curve where the rails ran between boulders and brush about seventy-five yards on from that point, in clear view, on a straight stretch of track. It would mean that the engineer would have to be alert and apply the brakes at once.

Then Billy Brett had remarked, 'Soon as it's done, we light out for the fresh animals.' He had shifted his gaze to Crane.

'That bay o' yourn, he'd been near to run out afore we come on yuh. He'll sure git stretched when we pull out o' here.'

Crane had asked, 'Where to?'

Yorke had answered that. 'Old way station, nor'-east o' here. Feller there owes me. This is a good time to square things.' Something else completely new to Crane. Clearly, so far, he had been told only what Sam Yorke wanted him to know. Among them, Crane was by no means seen as one of them. 'All these animals, they'll be run hard. We change 'em for fresh mounts.'

Crane, thinking quickly, had said, 'Nor'-east?'

Billy Brett had chuckled. Yorke had said, 'Back along the way the train come. Reckon they'll pick us headin' the other way, to the Holmans. So we'll make us a wide loop, then go south.'

Crane could see it then. They would end up not far from where Billy Brett had been before he found Crane himself. Go to ground. Wait it out. Old Sam Yorke playing another of his shrewd hands. In so many ways he was like Stoddart, you never knew what he might do next.

Now Yorke led them to the place where ultimately the South-western freight would be brought to a stop. Yorke, looking along the tracks to where the steel lines vanished around the curve, brush on either hand bunching so close that it must almost touch the sides of the train, raked fingers through his black beard. Then he paced out a further dozen strides, increasing the distance within which the train would have to be braked to a standstill.

Crane was trying to visualize the train as it would be, halted. He did not know its length and doubted that Yorke did, precisely. But Yorke had made allowances for a longish train. Those who were waiting for it would be in the cover of brush.

Crane, flicking glances around the group could sense the mounting interest. Even Goss, with his injured face, had been listening to Yorke with silent attention.

They had some food, then at Yorke's instruction they carefully checked the horses for soundness, checked their personal gear, the rifles, the pistols. It was an example of thoroughness which was surprising to Crane; even the usually casual Brett serious for once, going about these tasks single-mindedly and without comment.

Bob Teech had been talking with Yorke. Teech fetched a lariat, nodded to Goss and Geller. They had settled on a boulder that was partly buried in the earth, a lichen-covered stone about six feet in circumference. Teech dropped the noose over it. Teech, Goss and Geller, lariat over their shoulders, straining hard, made efforts to dislodge it. They could not. Crane joined them, then Brett. Bending to it, they got the boulder to lift slightly. Yorke came. All six grunted and heaved together. The boulder rolled free.

'Keep it comin'!' Yorke said. The big stone rolled, struck shiny steel track, resisted, then rolled over to settle between the rails. All but Teech let go the lariat. Teech coiled it and freed the loop.

Yorke nodded, hands on hips. He was looking again down the tracks to where they curved away beyond sight. 'Ready as we're ever gonna be.'

An hour later, Bob Teech, having mounted and walked his horse away out of their view, came bobbing back to them, all now mounted, waiting.

Teech merely nodded. He had seen the smudge of smoke against the sky. There was a general straightening and exchange of looks. They took the horses deep among brush, dismounted and tied the animals. Crane had been studying Yorke. A strange man, often keeping himself apart from the others. Scheming. Intelligent in his way. This observation had by no means offered Crane hope that, even now, he might be given an opportunity to put a pistol on the man, cut him out of the group. What had seemed possible in theory was a long way from that in reality. Now Crane was about to take part in a hold-up. What the consequences might be scarcely bore thinking about. Faintly, now, they could hear the approaching train.

Stoddart had had the glass on Hart this time. The old man was flabbergasted by what he had first thought he had seen, then by what the spyglass had confirmed. The wagon was here, too. Yet Stoddart could not see who was on it, or if there were others under its cover.

A short while back, a train, a freight he thought, had come along under rolling smoke, up a slight incline, come from the direction of Morland, heading south. Now Stoddart went back to where his horse was. He was some distance from Jesse Hart and the covered wagon, but now he had to make up his mind what to do. He was torn between looking further into Hart's activities and ranging south-westward, seeking some sign or word of

Abel Crane. He felt a stab of conscience when he thought of Crane. Stoddart blamed himself for what probably had happened to the man. Facing it squarely, it could be said that he had taken advantage of him. Used him. A man so badly in need of money would do almost anything to get his hands on some. The worst part was that Crane was not doing it for himself. And Stoddart had known that. Afterwards there might be those who would come forward and claim, justifiably, that Stoddart, a man with a fixation about Sam Yorke, had gone beyond all reason in one last attempt to rub out an old failure. Yorke, they would point out, had made him look like a fool. So he had been prepared to risk another man's neck to set matters right. Not for personal gain; for pride. So Stoddart brooded over Crane and came back to Jesse Hart. He tightened cinches he had earlier slacked off. He swung up into the smooth saddle, his old joints cracking.

They could hear the train now and see the thick smoke rolling away along its length, even though they were still among brush. And they were masked. Yorke had handed each man an oblong of white canvas with eyeholes cut in it, a thin strip of leather threaded along the top to tie it in place around the forehead. The mast hung below the jaw, giving the wearer a somewhat unnerving appearance, like some zombie risen from the grave.

Crane and Rudy Goss were armed with pistols. The others carried rifles. These four were also carrying burlap sacks, for the currency would likely be in small, canvas bank-sacks, awkward to carry away.

Now the locomotive, black and green and yellow, gushing smoke, was on the shallow curve, pistons working frantically, steam washing away on either side. Then the brakes were on. It seemed for a few seconds that the train would not be checked, even with locked wheels, skidding along the rails, the engineer in his blue

158

coveralls leaning from the cab. Then the whole thing was slowing, grindingly, steam billowing.

Crane thought he heard Billy Brett laugh. By the time the South-western freight ground to a stop, smoking, steaming, the clashing of its steel couplings stilled, the men were on the move.

Rudy Goss was climbing on to the platform of the locomotive. Crane, because he dare not do otherwise, was running along the length of the train towards the caboose. Yorke, Brett, Geller and Teech were walking into full view also, rifles in hand.

Aboard the train, the freight-conductor in his caboose, Praeger and Seligman, had been flung to the floor by the unexpected and severe braking. Baggage had fallen over and, elsewhere, freight had been dislodged. The freight-conductor having lost his cap, was still on hands and knees, looking for it when the rear door of the caboose was kicked in and a man wearing a white canvas mask and holding a pistol was suddenly inside.

Crane said, 'Get up!' The conductor's mouth had fallen open and his usually ruddy cheeks were drained of colour. The man was standing over him, repeating the instruction. Then, 'The Express car. Which?' Swallowing hard, the freight-conductor moved his round head slightly.

'Next 'un ...' Clearly he was not about to argue with a bandit holding a pistol.

Crane wagged the weapon. Out through the other door of the caboose they stepped to the end of the express car. Crane said, 'Have 'em open up. You can come out o' this still breathin'.'

For a few seconds the man stared at the eyes he could see through the holes in the canvas mask. It had been almost as though he had been told, *Here's a way out. No argument, no hurt.* The conductor rapped three times on the door. He was still staring at the masked bandit. They heard the bolts slide back. As soon as the door opened, Crane gave the conductor a shove in the back that sent the man bumping into another, a much older party with a thick white moustache and white hair. Praeger was still hatless.

The only other man in the express car was still on the floor and seemed to be having problems getting up again. He, too, was hatless and had a bald patch in the middle of his scalp, surrounded by a hedge of reddish hair. To the white-moustached man, Crane said, 'Make a move for that iron an' you'll get sent to your Maker. Open up the car.' Praeger made dampening motions with his hands, backing away. Seligman was getting up. Praeger stepped to the sliding doors at the side of the car and began unlocking them. Seligman got his first good look at the man wearing the unnerving canvas mask.

'Oh, Jesus!'

'Come to save you,' said Crane. 'Save you the trouble of takin' this stuff any further.' He moved his head towards the canvas sacks.

Seligman, licking dry lips, said, 'We'll get hung!' It seemed an unlikely outcome.

The white-moustached man had got the side door open to reveal, at the side of the track, four men masked like the one with the pistol, but all holding rifles. One of them, a thick black beard visible below his mask, stepped closer.

'Yuh got bank sacks in there! Toss 'em out!'

The man with the white moustache only hesitated for a second, then turned away to do it. But he did say, 'We know when we're outgunned, mister.' Indeed, the last thing on Praeger's mind, or Seligman's, was to resist. At that point, however, Bart Seligman did a stupid thing. He reached inside his coat for his silver flask. Crane had actually opened his mouth to yell at him, but was too late. Billy Brett it was, standing to the left of Sam Yorke, without lifting the rifle from hip-level, let go a smashing shot that whacked .44 lead into Saligman's side just beneath the left ribs, whence it drove upwards, distorting on its way, to lodge halfway up his right rib-cage. It flung him across the width of the car to finish up lying among the tumble of his own baggage, the flask he had been reaching for, skittering across the floor. Deep grunting noises were coming from Seligman, and Praeger, holding two bank sacks, would have released them and gone to him, but Yorke, springing up inside the car, stopped Praeger in his tracks.

'Leave the bastard. Git them sacks out.' Yorke himself handed his rifle to Crane and set about shoving canvas sacks into his own burlap one. The freight-conductor had not moved since preceding Crane into the car, but now turned aside, vomiting. The sour smell soon invaded the car.

Praeger was tossing small sacks outside. Others were picking them up, but not Billy Brett. He had his rifle lined up on the man with the white moustache.

Presently, Yorke said, 'That's it. Let's go.' Crane handed him his rifle and with that in one hand and the burlap sack in the other, Yorke jumped down out of the open car.

Crane backed around the old man, still holding his pistol on him and called to Yorke, 'I'll leave when you're clear!'

Nobody answered. All went jogging away into the brush. Crane caught a glimpse of Rudy Goss following them.

Praeger was now with the groaning Seligman, getting the coat off him, tearing at his shirt. 'Jesus!' It looked like a real bad one. The freight-conductor was still as pale as a man could be. He looked as though he might easily throw up again.

The horses were coming. Crane left the car, jumping to the ground as Bob Teech came riding up, leading Crane's bay. Some six minutes had elapsed since the South-western freight had come to its grinding halt.

Eleven

Right or wrong, Stoddart had made a decision. There would come a payment for that, a reckoning. Stoddart had no doubt of it. What form it might take, of course, he could not know, but he had to assume that it might also involve Crane, and to Crane's cost. Crane and his sick woman. Delia. As time went on, she was much in Stoddart's mind. On his conscience. She had been the sole reason for Crane's involvement in it. But Delia had not believed in Stoddart and had made no secret of it. Yet she had lacked the energy to do anything about it.

Even so, these things on his mind, he had all but allowed Jesse Hart to slip away. Hart might simply have vanished had it not been for the presence of the wagon. It had become clear that the horseman was to ride along with it, and for good reason, for it was carrying what he had gathered. Hart. Stoddart thought about the man. Was he deluding himself that if the time came, he could ever hope to take the man? Later it would be said that he was foolhardy. So be it. He knew it already.

If Billy Brett had foretold a hard ride he had not been understating the case. They were all away, their masks discarded, the rising tower of smoke from the stationary South-western well behind them.

Billy was leading out now, quirting his horse, stretching it out, the wide brim of his hat flattened with the wind of his riding. Yorke came next, then Bob Teech, Jack Geller, then Crane and, tailing them, clearly still in pain, Rudy Goss. So engrossed did they become in their flight from the train, that things that otherwise would have been noticed, went unseen. A rise of dust across to their left, then the specks of riders moving under it. In fact it was Goss, at the back, who first noticed them and began yelling. They heard him and looked. Finally, Billy Brett and Sam Yorke, joining up, waved the others to a halt, the horses tossing heads and screwing about.

Then someone among the oncoming riders, one who, as they drew closer, must have recognized clothing, or an attitude, the set of a certain horseman, let go a smoky pistol shot. The unlikely had come to pass. What these men wanted, Rudy Goss was sitting on: the Diamond L horse.

Rifles were unsheathed and levered. Yorke and Brett slammed shots away. One among the other riders shot back with a rifle, the lead humming close to Crane. The ranch riders—five—were not astride cow-ponies but saddlers, and they had done well, thought Crane, to track their stolen animal as well as they had. They had been underestimated. Even if they did not know who they were up against, however, they found out quite soon that it was not going to be easy.

Sam Yorke split his party into two. He, Brett and Geller went bounding away together in the direction they had been riding. Crane, Teech and Goss doubled back and to their left, both parties shooting with rifles. As might have been expected, the Diamond L all came at one group of three, the one Crane was in as it happened, obviously seeking to overwhelm it with greater numbers. Then Yorke's party suddenly changed direction, cutting left, shooting and threatening to get in behind the ranch riders. Someone among the Diamond L was fly enough to see what would happen should they get caught between the two lots of shooters. As one, the Diamond L hesitated. That was to be the cowmen's undoing.

Suddenly Sam Yorke, Brett and Geller were coming right at them hard. Then Bob Teech, alongside Crane, tracking a ranch rider with his rifle, shot and hit the man. The cowboy was whacked back and up out of the saddle and fell. That set the others turning, milling in obvious confusion. One swung down to help the one who had been shot.

Yorke and his party went veering away. Crane, Teech and Goss, shooting at the cowmen—Crane firing high—cut around and resumed their earlier line of ride, Yorke slowing, waiting for them, Billy Brett cussing and saying he had never believed the cowmen would have had the wit to track him, and by God, if there had been time he would have given the bastards a whole lot more to think about. Yorke's party went rowelling away, this time quirting the horses to even greater effort. It was clear that Yorke did not want to leave anything to chance, wanting to be quit of this part of the country as soon as may be. In the urgencies of the robbery and flight afterwards, the presence of Abel Crane had seemingly engaged fewer minds, even Rudy Goss concentrating on getting clear. Maybe he just thought that Crane would keep.

On they rode, the animals now showing some signs of flagging. But Yorke would not let up, no doubt the certainty of fresh mounts causing him to care less about the ones they had now. As for Crane himself, he had feelings which troubled him, caught up as he was with these notorious and dangerous men. Things had gone wrong—for all Yorke's planning—and the results could not be put right. The shooting of the man at the Diamond L, the shooting of another in the express car, and now the cowboy back there, all without compunction, as though those doing the shooting had been engaged in little more than killing flies. And he, Crane, had been part of it.

Impatient as Yorke was, they were compelled to spell the horses. The animals could run no more. But soon enough they were away again, albeit at a reduced pace, pressing on towards the abandoned way station. It was under a darkening sky that Yorke, now leading, called, 'That's it, boys!'

There was a spark of light about a mile ahead of them.

The small covered wagon and the single rider came out between a clay bluff and a cluster of weather-smooth boulders to find a mounted man sitting quite still on his black horse, a rifle cradled across his front. Horseman and wagon came to a halt.

The black-coated man, Hart, moved a hand, unbuttoned the coat, but before he could lay a hand on the exposed handle of the pistol, Stoddart called, 'Don't touch it, Jesse!'

Hart seemed to lean forward slightly in the saddle as though the better to see the rifleman who had called him by his given name. Then he sat back again, his face betraying no emotion whatsoever, nothing to give away what he might have been thinking. Then he said, 'Ed Stoddart.' A pause. 'Been a right long time, Ed.'

'Not near long enough, Jesse.' Stoddart nudged the black with his knees, walking it a few yards closer. Now he was pointing the rifle in the general direction of the horseman. It could have been half an invitation for Hart to make a try for the pistol. If it was, Hart did not accept it.

Stoddart was looking at the wagon. The driver had on a wide-brimmed hat and some kind of thick coat and was looking down rather than at Stoddart. Hart said, 'Be advisable to stand aside, Ed. I got business elsewhere.'

'Don't doubt that,' said Stoddart. Holding the rifle in one big, rawboned hand, with the other he reached to one of his saddle-bags and brought out the brass spyglass. Then he put it away again. 'Fetched yuh in close, Jesse. Got to take a look in the wagon.'

Hart said nothing, but watched, stony-faced, as Stoddart now walked the black horse forward and eventually came around behind Hart, reached and unthonged the hammer of Hart's pistol and drew it from the holster. He tossed it some forty feet away. Stoddart shuffled the black backwards to put reasonable distance between himself and Jesse Hart. He considered it to be a rational action. Now he turned his attention to the wagon and its driver.

'Look at me,' Stoddart said.

The driver looked first towards Hart, then at the man with the rifle. Stoddart's brows went up. The driver was a woman. With the wide-brimmed hat on and the coat—which had a large collar turned up at the back—she had looked like a youngish man. But when Stoddart got a clearer view he saw that she must be in her late thirties.

He said, 'Step down.'

Again she cast a glance at Hart, who nodded, and she wound the lines around the brake lever and climbed down. Now

Stoddart could also see that she had on a pair of man's pants made of worsted material. The woman stood alongside the wagon.

'Stay right there, ma'am,' Stoddart said. 'Got to take a look in this here rig o' yourn.' Stoddart walked the horse around the back of the rig, swung down, allowing the reins to hang, and approached the wagon. Whatever had occupied Jesse Hart for a good long while, earlier, had been put in this vehicle. The mistake that Stoddart made was one that, earlier in his career, he would have warned others about. Because he was dealing with a woman, to a degree he allowed his defences to lower. He had never set eyes on this particular woman before, so her name would have meant nothing to him. If he had in fact known anything of Lola Barrett he would not have taken her so cheaply.

Just as he had got one foot up on the iron step at the back of the rig, the woman walked around to where he was and, having taken it from a capacious pocket of her coat, was holding an old Merwin and Hulbert .44 in her right hand and gripping, with her left hand, the right wrist for additional support. The pistol was cocked. As soon as Stoddart turned his head he knew she was going to shoot him, and at that instant, in a spurt of fire and smoke, she did, the pistol bucking in her hand.

Stoddart was punched hard by the large calibre lead, and fell off the wagon-step, losing his rifle in the process. Stoddart hit the ground heavily, his hat rolling away. Lola Barrett did not fire again, but returned to the front of the wagon and climbed back on the seat. She unwound the lines from the brake lever. Hart, still mounted, went looking for his pistol. By the time he located it, dismounted and remounted, the wagon was rolling again. Hart glanced back at the fallen Stoddart, perhaps in two minds about going to him or following the wagon. After that brief hesitation he knee'd the horse and followed the wagon.

Stoddart's black horse had given a couple of bounds away, then stopped, shook its head and came walking back to observe Stoddart who, since striking the ground, had not moved. He was bleeding badly. The first numbing blow of the ball was fading to be replaced by intense pain. Grunting, breathing harshly, one large hand pressed to his right side, Stoddart reached out with the other, found he was short, began inching forward, sweat slick on him, until his fingers touched the Winchester. Blinking his eyes against the gathering sweat, Stoddart now brought his bloodied right hand forward and, with an agonizing effort, raked the rifle to him, to be grasped in both hands. He got the thick stickiness of blood on the stock and the sideplates and trigger-guard, his broad fingers slipping as he struggled to support himself on his elbows. His vision was swimming and for several seconds he was compelled to rest his forehead on the rifle.

Still labouring, Stoddart lifted his eyes, blinking them, and somehow drew the butt-plate of the Winchester against his right shoulder.

Jesse Hart, bobbing alongside the wagon, was now a good distance away. Stoddart was doing his utmost to line up the diminishing figure in the black coat. The rifle was wavering, his heavy breathing not assisting him. Again Stoddart rested his head, then raised it. He brought every ounce of his strength and concentration to bear, a bloodied forefinger curled around the trigger. He reckoned he would get but one shot. He would never be able to summon the strength to reload.

The lash of Stoddart's rifle sounded flatly on the still air. He did not know whether or not he had hit Jesse Hart, but there was a suggestion that the man's horse had gone skipping sideways before darkness descended on the shooter.

In the gloom, beyond some outbuildings, they could see several horses in a corral. The principal building was a split-log structure with a low-pitched roof, poled overhangs on all sides. It was this building that was showing yellowish lamplight. Somebody there had come out carrying a lantern. Yorke swung down, tossed the reins to Geller and called, 'Git them others saddled!' He walked forward to speak to the man who had come out while Crane and the others all headed for the corral. A dozen horses were in there but there would be no time to pick and choose.

'Jes' drop a rope on the nearest,' Billy Brett advised. 'Culver claimed they'd all be good mounts.'

Crane, passing Billy as he said it, almost stopped in his tracks. He made the effort to pass on by. *Culver*. To believe that it would not be the Culver he feared it would be, would be folly. Jase Culver. In an enterprise such as this, it was highly likely. The shock of it had almost driven the breath from him. After all this time and at this remote place, Jase Culver. If that man were to hear the name Abel Crane, or merely catch a glimpse, it would be all over. His mouth dry and his heart pounding in his chest, Crane, leading the spent bay, arrived at the corral. Some of the party, vague figures, were already standing with looped lariats.

Twelve

Afterwards Stoddart would be hard put to it to remember how he had managed to get back on the horse. Now he was sitting the saddle but none too securely. A folded bandanna was wadded under his much-bloodied shirt against the entry wound in his side. The bleeding had diminished, but Stoddart sure was a sick man.

The wagon and Jesse Hart had vanished long ago into a gathering gloom, for now it was past sundown. From time to time the reap-hook moon was veiled by drifting clouds. On his walking horse, Stoddart was headed more or less southwest, though he could scarcely have said why. Some vague, pain-racked notion to be in that part of the country where Abel Crane might still be. The hell with Jesse Hart was one thought.

Maybe it had been a bad mistake to allow himself to be diverted by that man. Well, he had well and truly paid for it. Stoddart did not know who the hell the woman had been, but it had turned out she was fit companion for Jesse Hart. Stoddart liked to believe that he had hit the man with the rifle shot. Wearily he shook his head in an effort to clear it. What the hell did it matter now? Yet what came back to goad Stoddart was the glimpse he had caught of what the wagon had contained seen, only moments before the .44 ball hit him.

Crane had got his lariat on a fresh horse and had tied the animal to a pole of the corral. He loosed the cinches and lifted the saddle off the bay. First, he dumped the heavy kak and transferred the blanket from one horse to the other. He was one of the last to settle on a fresh horse and set about shifting his gear, only Bob Teech with him at the corral. The others had gone strolling across to the sprawling main building of the old way station.

Teech said, 'Sam, he'll pay off Jase Culver an' we'll be on our way.' Clearly they were not to tarry for any longer than necessary at this place. Yorke's policy of taking no chances. Hollowly, Crane heard it confirmed that the man at the way station *was* Jase Culver. There was only one chance that could fall Crane's way. If his name was not mentioned and he kept himself well out of the way, he might just get away with it. The rest of them had gone inside the building. They would be wanting to at least get a look at the currency in the sacks out of the express car. Crane secured his saddle, then his bedroll, set his saddle-bags and put his lariat on the chosen horse, another bay, as it happened.

Sam Yorke was indeed getting ready to pay off Jase Culver for his fresh horses and the risks he was taking. Geller, Brett and Goss were arriving in the way station to get themselves a first look at the haul they had got.

It had been Crane's intention to make some excuse not to go near where the light was, but Bob Teech, having got his own fresh mount ready, and with Crane's, led it out of the corral and light-hitched it near the others, now said to him, 'Let's go on in an' take us a look at what we got.'

Crane began walking with him. They had not advanced far, however, before hearing the sounds coming from inside the building, sounds which clearly were an eruption of rage and frustration. It was so violent as to cause even Bob Teech to hesitate, then stop. Crane stopped. In the dark, not yet come into the spill of light from the window, Crane's right hand had grasped the handle of the pistol. He thumbed the thong from the hammer. Yet the reason for the sudden outburst had not been because of him.

Jack Geller, in impotent fury, could be seen in the long oblong of lighted doorway. His hands were full of crumpled paper. Some of it Geller balled tightly and flung to the floor. Other pieces went fluttering away. What the problem was had become all too clear even to those outside the building. The canvas sacks that they had taken from the express car of the South-western had not been filled with bank bills: they had been stuffed with soft paper of the size of bank bills.

Walking back and forth Sam Yorke now came into view. He seemed almost transported with fury. Bob Teech started forward again just as Yorke yelled, 'Bob! Abel!' Though Crane himself did not hear it, Jase Culver must have picked up a name that was new to him, making *'Abel? Who the hell's Abel?'*

Crane stopped. After what Crane thought was only a few seconds, Yorke's voice came again. 'Bob? Fetch Crane in here ...' *Bounty hunter.*

Bob Teech was turning and in the act of opening his mouth when Crane drawing his pistol, lifted it and brought the long barrel hard down on Teech's neck. Teech staggered, his hat falling, and Crane struck him again. He turned and ran through the darkness.

Crane was nearing the corral when from somewhere behind him at the way station, came the first stab of flame and the sound of a pistol. He had no sense of lead passing close to him. Someone called, perhaps warning the shooter against risking a hit on one of the horses. Crane arrived at the horse he had saddled, whipping the reins free from the corral-pole. The horse had been startled by the man running through the dark, tossing its head and going sidling away. Crane, one foot in the stirrup, went hopping after the animal, cursing. By the time he managed to swing a leg over the cantle and got settled in the saddle, he could hear others coming. And they were wasting no time.

Crane hauled the horse away and put spurs to it and sent it bounding forward. Another pistol banged. This time the lead came breathing close to him as he rode on out into the deeper darkness. Crane did not answer them in kind. He did not want to disclose his whereabouts with pistol-flare. But he did not doubt that some of them at least would come out after him in jig-time. Having been obviously double-crossed by the men on the train, they would now want to spend some of their fury on Abel Crane's own deceit. All the half-suspicions had suddenly borne fruit. They had been taken in and made to look fools, especially Billy Brett. Now Crane could but hope that the horse beneath him, which had seemed robust enough, had a good long run in it.

A rifle cracked. That made the fleeing rider's skin crawl, even though the bullet had not come near him. A shot on the fly. Crane rode on, trusting the horse to find safe passage between clumps of brush. A cloud went sliding from the hooked moon. The greater light brought two further lashing shots from rifles behind him, and this time the bullets came whipping dangerously close to him. He passed in and out of a small *arroyo,* and by the time he emerged, the moon was screened by cloud again. As he rode, the images of Jack Geller and Sam Yorke came back at him, bellowing their anger. *Duped. Made to look fools.* Those aboard the South-western must have *known* that Yorke, or someone, was set to stop the train. The old bastard with the white moustache and the fool who had got himself shot reaching for a flask, must surely have prepared the false bank-sacks, made the switch, the false sacks carried in the baggage that had been there in the express car. But at what *risk?* If Yorke or any one of them had chosen to take a look inside one of the sacks, there would have been instant killing, trying to find the currency. Right at the start the lie had been fed to Bob Teech. Crane would not have given a wooden dime for the chances of that man's survival in the face of Sam Yorke's wrath. That he had thought out but half of the deceit, Crane could not know. He went hammering through the night, the pack still baying at his heels.

Stoddart had got himself down off the horse and had managed to picket the animal and then to get a fire going. Bathed in sweat, he had made coffee and was now sipping it, trying to restore himself with it, at least to some extent. The ugly wound had dried and his entire side had stiffened. And he was still carrying the .44 lead deep inside him. His lungs were functioning, but each breath that he took was a refinement of mere pain.

Slowly Stoddart turned his old face this way, then that. A shit of a place to finish up in. But he had spent the greater part of his life alone, so there was nothing new in that; a young bride gone early, pinned by her swan's throat to a yard door by a Sioux arrow. That was so long ago that now it seemed like another lifetime entirely.

Stoddart, however, was having trouble focusing and keeping his thoughts in order. He was surer, now, that he had hit the black-coated man. Or was he merely wishing it to be true? There had been occasions during the past painful hours when he had seen that he had been mistaken, that Jesse Hart had been unscathed and, in fact, had come back with the purpose of killing Stoddart. The strange thing was that Hart had never been there; only the vast, silent land, the rocks and the raking brush. Once, he had seen Abel Crane, but that, too, had been an illusion, for he had turned into Delia Crane, with her sunken, milk-white face. Blinking his eyes had released him from her. Only to be confronted with Royce Praeger. How he regretted now that he had not taxed Jesse Hart with that piece of knowledge. The fire flickered and he closed his eyes.

In the first minutes of the pale dawn, they had got Crane boxed in among some boulders, the passages between which were almost choked with vegetation. It was possible to keep out of sight for most of the time, him and the horse, but he was no longer going anywhere.

A change of direction had proved to be a mistake, for one of them—he thought it had been Jack Geller—had managed by some means to get ahead of him. Two others, Billy Brett and Rudy Goss were the ones at his back. As far as Crane could discover, Sam Yorke was not of the party who had come out after him, nor Jase Culver, nor Bob Teech, who was likely in no shape to ride anywhere, so hard had Crane struck him.

Crane had dismounted now, crouching, ducking away instinctively as rifle fire lashed out and lead came cutting the air close over his head from two different quarters. He was not given time to think about his predicament, for one of the men now besieging him and who had dismounted, must have got in a lot closer than Crane had thought possible. The rifle shot sounded very loudly. Crane himself was not hit, but the horse was rearing and screaming and then, tearing free of the brush that Crane had tied it to, went crashing to the ground. It began kicking and rolling and screaming, quivering. Crane crawled to it and shot the animal between the eyes, then went rolling away.

He crouched and waited. All had fallen quiet. They knew that he was going nowhere in a hurry. They were on two sides at least, perhaps three. It was but a matter of time. Crane swivelled his head peering this way and that. The silence ran on.

Suddenly he saw Jack Geller running across an open space. It was unexpected, but as it turned out Geller was unlucky, for Crane, gripping his rifle in both hands, took a fly shot, a touch ahead of the man, and hit him. Geller veered sharply away as though actually pushed by the heavy lead, arms flailing, to vanish among vegetation.

Billy Brett and Rudy Goss were at that

time working closer in, but from opposite directions, and it was Crane now who had to go hugging the ground, back to where the horse lay, and he prepared to fort up behind it. The trouble was that because of the boulders and brush, if they pressed forward with care, they could be on him before he realized they were coming.

Then he heard Billy say, 'Jack?' Clearly, they did not know that Geller had been hit. Another period of quietness fell. A small breeze sprang up, and with it, lifts of dust. The big danger, Crane thought, was Billy. Goss might be a hard man (now, perhaps, not as hard as he might have imagined) but he did not have the cunning of Billy Brett. The difference between Brett and Goss was what now, in this desperate situation, Crane made up his mind he must work on.

So he called out to Goss, 'C'mon Rudy ... hard man. Come blow me away ...'

Almost immediately, Crane heard Brett's voice, not laughing now, saying something, though he could not hear what. But he guessed that it was a warning from the sharp-minded Brett to the big man not to be goaded into doing something stupid. But, by God, they must be close.

Crane thought that he had to make things happen, for he could not afford to be pinned down here. If he did, then sooner or later they would be bound to nail him. Brett and Goss could scarcely have failed to hear the ruckus and see the dust rising when the horse had been shot. They would have worked out that he would try to fort up behind it. So to get a sight of the horse would be to pinpoint where the man was. Crane thought he had better do something about that. There was an almost eerie sense of their close presence.

Crane had been inching forward on both his elbows while still holding his rifle, leaving behind him in the dust a faint slug-trail. In this slow, laborious fashion he had advanced some five yards, then stopped. He was surprised to be looking full at Rudy Goss. The man was only a matter of twenty yards from him. Crane let go a shot and saw it whack home in Goss's left shoulder. Goss disappeared. Crane retreated fast. He could hear Goss yelling. Then the sounds stopped.

Maybe ten minutes went by before Crane heard the next sounds. These were the clinking of bit-chains and the whickering of horses. Crane's first reaction was that it was some kind of trick, but he had to find out what was going on. He went edging forward again, listening to the horses, the occasional sound of a voice. He began to believe that they really were pulling out. Evidently they had given up on Jack Geller, maybe having discovered that he was dead.

There was no doubt at all that horses were on the move. Then Crane saw them, Billy Brett and Rudy Goss, Goss swaying in the saddle, riding away, leading a third horse. Geller's. They passed behind tall brush, then re-emerged further away.

Pulling out right enough. Still not quite accepting it, Crane continued watching through narrowed eyes as the slow-moving horsemen diminished. One dead, one hit. No sign of Sam Yorke. When he was sure that they were still moving along without looking back, and were a good distance away, he began to relax. Well, Billy had been fly enough to take Jack Geller's horse along, denying it to Crane.

Crane went to his own dead animal and spent some time dragging all his gear off it. This he stashed among brush, apart from his canteen, though God knew when he might be able to get back here to retrieve it. Then, rifle in hand, and his canteen slung by a thong around his neck, he set out afoot, heading vaguely in the direction of where he thought the railroad tracks to be. If he could make it to there he would have a sure direction for the town of Morland.

As the sun climbed higher in the sky, he found progress more difficult, but he knew that if he were to stop, he might lose the will to go on again. From time to time he looked behind him but there was no sign of dust that might have foretold riders. After a couple of hours, squinting in the day's brightness, he brushed a hand across his eye and stopped. Some hundred yards further on, among rocks and beyond some scrappy brush, there was a faint rise of smoke. Crane moved on, but circumspectly, keeping his attention on it, listening for any sound that might confirm the presence of men, for this was clearly a camp-fire. It might be smoking only faintly but in this country nobody would have ridden away and left any life whatsoever in a fire. Very cautiously he came to the camp.

Ed Stoddart was in a bad way, though still sitting upright and still capable of recognizing Abel Crane.

Thirteen

Crane had done what he could for the old man. It did not amount to much. Bathed the wound but not bound it.

'No use,' Stoddart had said, in a now very forced voice. And they had traversed (in Stoddart's case, in somewhat halting words at times) what was known about Sam Yorke and Billy Brett and about Jesse Hart. And the woman who had put a bullet in Stoddart. No blame being laid. No recriminations. The risks had been plain enough from the outset. Yet there was some regret.

'Old fool,' Stoddart remarked of himself.

Crane shrugged. 'Give you up for dead, almost.'

'Come to that, near as dammit. Yuh reckon Billy's gone?'

Again, Crane shrugged. 'Not in Billy's nature.' Then, 'Sooner or later, he'll come. Sam, too, maybe.'

Stoddart thought about it. 'Got to give up on Yorke, Abel. You're but one man. Now they know what's what. Best yuh git after Jesse. He's where the sure money is.' The implication was plain enough, but Crane did not pick up on it.

Instead he asked, 'You worked out what went on?'

Stoddart ran his tongue between dry, bluish lips. 'I do know Jesse Hart an' that woman, they got bank sacks in that wagon ... Watched Jesse collectin' 'em up all along the rail tracks, on an incline ... few mile this side o' Sour Creek.'

Crane said, 'In that express car there was a lot o' baggage. The two in there with it had to have switched the sacks, dumped the money for Hart to pick up, let ol' Sam Yorke take the paper. Yorke got to know about the shipment. Feller named Bob Teech got that from a woman. Lola

Barrett. By God, they took one hell of a chance that Sam would make the raid. An' if he did, they'd get away with the switch. For sheer brass you got to give 'em a nod.'

Blinking, Stoddart said huskily, 'Lola Barrett, she'd be the one ...' He indicated his wounded side. Then he asked, 'One o' the fellers in that express car, an old 'un? White moustaches?'

'He was. There was another. Seligman. He was a fool. He got shot. Him, white moustaches, Hart, they must've been all in it together. An' the woman. Who's white moustaches?'

'Royce Praeger,' Stoddart said. 'Marshalled with Royce, one time ... a while back, now. Saw 'im meet up with Jesse Hart ... Couldn't git over that.' Then he told Crane the direction the wagon had gone and how long ago. 'Ain't gonna make good time.'

Crane thought about it, then said, 'Praeger, he could wait a good long while

201

for his cut.'

'Like ... forever,' Stoddart said, with the wintriest of smiles. And he came back to what he had said a little earlier, but with greater emphasis, as though if he did not get it said now, he might never do so. And maybe to say, without saying, that his fixation with Sam Yorke could no longer be justified in any way. Crane had given it the best try he could. No man could ask him to do more. 'South-western an' the bank ... they'll pay out good, Abel ... yuh got to git out after Jesse.' And before Crane could say anything, he added, 'Yuh don't jes' owe it to yourself ...' There was Delia. She was at the centre of it. The reason for Crane's being here at all. 'Git on that ... horse o' mine, Abel, an' ... go find Jesse.'

Crane said, 'There's a real good chance Brett'll come.' He still believed that Billy had ridden away too readily, even with Goss wounded. 'Can't leave you out here, Ed.'

If Stoddart had had the energy to summon it, maybe there would have been genuine anger. 'Either way ... I ain't goin' nowheres. I know it an' you know it. So jes' git aboard that there animal an' go. Leave me this pistol an' jack a fresh load in the Winchester, 'case I can't git it done.' His head sank down. Crane did as he was bid and in a few minutes he had mounted up. He walked the black horse around the perimeter of Stoddart's camp, having doused the fire. Finally he paused. 'I'll be back, Ed.'

'There's a spyglass in the saddle-bag. Yuh might need it. Git gone.'

With a breeze at his back. Crane headed on out, soon working the black into a good canter, a pace that, once settled into, would eat up the miles. He felt coldly angry and heartsick at the same time. After a while, coming to some rising ground, slowing the horse, Crane's head lifted and he drew the animal to a halt. Then he turned it around, to sit as still as he could, straining to hear the faint sounds that had come to him on the following breeze. There, again. One ... two ... three. A pause, then a fourth sound. Gunfire. Way back there. Crane knew it would be pointless to obey an impulse to go back. There came a fifth shot, then no more. That was indeed, the one Billy Brett had fired, that had blown the top of old Stoddart's head away.

Crane found the wagon stopped near the bank of a wandering creek, a green place, some cottonwoods, some juniper, a lot of deep bunch-grass. He did not need to use Stoddart's spyglass to observe that Jesse Hart, a man in a black coat, was still with the woman, Lola Barrett. They were in the process of gathering dry sticks for a fire.

Crane was beyond any thoughts of subtlety. Old Stoddart's face was too clear in his mind. Anyway Hart must have seen him coming, and even if he had not, must have heard the levering of the Winchester, for the man, turning fast, made a dive for the pistol that apparently he had laid aside for some reason. Because Hart was moving quickly Crane did not attempt to shoot at him. Even when Hart snatched at shellbelt, holster and pistol and with them, went rolling quickly away, Crane still held back. He was closing the distance to the camp, the black walking. Only when Hart, having unthonged the hammer of the pistol and was drawing it from the holster did Crane pull the horse to a stop. Rifle to his shoulder, he let go a cracking shot.

Jesse Hart took the belting lead in the chest, his pistol discharging into the ground. He was knocked backwards. Crane, levering fast, lined up and shot him again, Hart's prone body jumping from the impact of the hit.

Crane, levering the rifle, yelled to the woman, 'Drop it! Let it go!' She had got hold of a pistol, probably the one she had shot Stoddart with. For the space of a few seconds, he thought she might try to defy the odds. She had actually got the pistol in her hands. She was staring at the lanky, unshaven, mounted man squinting along the barrel of his rifle. The range was about sixty feet. She must have seen that her life was hanging by the merest thread. She got that confirmed when he said, 'I found the US deputy marshal. He wasn't dead then. No doubt that he is, now. That's down to you, lady.' Lola uncocked the pistol and let it fall into the grass. Crane came forward, dismounted, picked the weapon up. A Merwin and Hulbert .44. He carried it with him when he went to the wagon, stepped up and looked inside. Briefly. He saw what old Stoddart had seen at the instant he was shot. Crane stepped down and looked at the woman. Her attention was now on the fallen Jesse Hart.

He said, 'Go anywhere near the weapons he had an' I'll recall Ed Stoddart an' forget you're female.' She gave him a flat, expressionless look. He had to ask,

'You an' Jesse Hart, you were away, just the two of you. What about them on the train?' He moved his head to indicate the wagon. 'The ones who threw the sacks off? Seligman an' Praeger?' It was apparent that he had surprised her with the names.

'Who the hell *are* you?'

Crane shook his head. 'Not important. Well?'

She drew in a long breath. 'It was Bart Seligman an' Royce Praeger. It was their scheme. Seligman fed it to me, made out it was careless doin' that. They figured I'd pass it on to a feller called Bob Teech an' from there it would go straight to Sam Yorke. It was bait, for Sam. He took it.'

'Hart?'

'He was the third one. What they didn't know was that me an' Jesse, we ... went back a long way.' So old white moustaches had been deceived as well. Crane had to smile sourly.

He said, 'So the boys in the express car made the change. Sam took the bait an' the paper. They took one hell of a risk. Sam Yorke robbed the South-western. As far as the bank would ever know, that's where their money had gone.'

She nodded, looking weary now. 'They worked out where Yorke would likely hit the train. They'd dump the money before that.'

'An' Sam, he could hardly complain about what he found in the sacks he got.' Then he said, 'Climb up on the wagon.'

'Where we headed?'

'Morland, to start with.'

She said, 'Reckon they'll pay you real well for this, mister.'

'They will,' Crane said, 'but it'll have been earned. Old Ed Stoddart, he got nothin' but a lead ball. He didn't deserve that.'

She said nothing. It was going to seem a hell of a long way to Morland. Crane stood back while she prepared to get up on the wagon-seat. Then his head lifted and the woman turned her face to look at him. Horsemen were coming. He could hear the blowing of the animals and the clinking of bit-chains.

Fourteen

Crane said to her, 'I hear 'em but I can't see 'em yet.' Then, 'We can't run. There'd be no point. You can choose what you want to do. I've got no choice but to make a stand.'

'Who are they?'

'Billy Brett for one. Likely a man called Culver. Maybe even Sam Yorke.' He could see that had hit her hard.

She said, 'Let me have the pistol. I don't want to stand here waitin' to get shot.'

He gave her the Merwin and Hulbert. 'Jesse, he had a rifle.'

'I'll go get it.' Hurrying, she did. By that time Crane had unhitched the wagon-horses.

'Now, get in under the wagon. Better

hope you can shoot at moving targets. When these boys get a sight of the sacks in that wagon, you wouldn't want to be still here an' alive.' He thought that such would be the case, anyway, for they were outnumbered and by some real hard-noses. So if it came out badly, when they had finished with her, they would burn her, in the wagon.

Then here they were, Brett, Culver and, indeed, Sam Yorke. Of Goss there was no sign and Crane had expected none. It took them a few seconds to absorb what was here and who was here. As soon as they did, they spread out fast and got themselves into some sort of cover among the cottonwoods and brush. Culver had some problems with his horse and soon had to abandon it and get himself down out of sight.

Crane and Lola Barrett were under the wagon, which was standing in deep bunch-grass. The wagon-horses had drifted away. Somebody fired a rifle and there was a *whapping* sound as lead went whipping through canvas.

Crane said, 'Pretty soon they'll commence working the target. There'll be a lot of lead coming in on the wagon. Use your elbows, follow me, crawl real slow through the grass towards the creek. Ten yards, that's what we need.' Now she realized why Crane had set the wagon-horses loose, drawing attention to the vehicle itself, standing in long grass. A throw of the dice. Yorke might be too old a dog to swallow it, but there was not much else, no other card to play.

As Crane went inching away, out from under the wagon, he was doing his utmost to avoid causing a disturbance as he moved through the grass. Lola Barrett, albeit with more difficulty, was tracking him closely.

Rifle fire lashed out again. Lead went *spanging* off metal as the wagon was struck repeatedly. Crane, followed by the woman, went edging down the slight slope towards the creek. Another rifle shot came and there was a rap as the wagon took another hit. There must now be some puzzlement amoung the Yorke party about the complete lack of answering fire.

Crane uttered, 'Don't shoot on the fly. Sooner or later we got to give 'em some back, but only when there's something to shoot at. Soon as we do, they'll know we've quit that wagon.' The sharp crack of rifle-fire all but buried the last couple of words. More shots, one ... two ... three ... four. Methodical shooting, repeatedly hitting the wagon and tearing through bunch-grass beneath it. Crane thought it could not go on much longer without Yorke twigging that he was shooting at a dead target. Crane began to think that his own chance would never come. Then it did.

There was a slight disturbance, one of the wagon-horses having gone ambling closer to some cottonwoods down to Crane's left, lifting its head, trotting through deep grass here, heading away. Then, Crane, now hatless, raised his eyes and saw a small patch of colour. Blue. A shirt. He tried to recall, in the brief sighting he had got earlier, which of them had been wearing a blue shirt. He thought maybe it had been Culver.

Propping on elbows, sighting carefully, Crane, judging the distance to be seventy feet, lined up. When his aim settled, he held his breath and squeezed the trigger. The Winchester lashed and instantly there was the crisp smack of a hit and a flurry of disturbed branches and blue shirt, then nothing. No cry. All sounds ceased except the blowing of horses.

Then a voice, Billy's, called 'Jase?' No response came. Crane, lying quite still now, tried to work out where the call had come from. He heard a brief exchange between Billy and Sam Yorke, but could not hear what was said. Then silence fell again. After maybe half a minute a rifle went off and the bullet came slashing through the bunch-grass mere feet from where Crane and the woman were lying. The fat was sure in the fire now. They had got away with all they were going to.

Now, suddenly there was movement. Crane could not at first see who was moving or where. Then Lola Barrett said, 'On the other side of the wagon.'

Then Crane saw Sam Yorke. The black-bearded man had clearly had enough and had made up his mind to finish it fast. He was running through the deep grass, rifle at hip, coming right at where Crane and the woman were. Then, from near the wagon, Billy began firing.

Lola, using Hart's Winchester, shot back at Billy. Crane fired quickly at the oncoming Sam Yorke and missed him. A bullet ripped through grass close to Crane's head. Again he shot at Yorke and thought he had missed him a second time, but was surprised when after another stride, the bearded man went down on his knees. At first the shock of the bullet seemed not to have impeded him, such was the insensate fury of his approach, all guile gone, all reason, all care.

Suddenly Crane rose and fired towards the wagon and began jogging towards it, seeing Billy there by the side of it, pressing fresh loads in. Shooting as he ran, Crane yelled 'Too goddamn' late, Billy!' Then he saw that Brett had cast the rifle aside and the big eye of a .44 was coming up and blasting fire and smoke.

But Crane shot him with the rifle and there was a slap like an axe striking a melon as Billy was head-shot, red spray flying, going over on his back to lie still in the long grass.

Crane heard Lola scream, 'Yorke!' and he turned even as Yorke's rifle blasted, yet the black-bearded man fell forward. Crane walked to him. Sam Yorke was staring out of sightless eyes. Crane turned his head and called to the woman, 'He's done for!' She did not answer.

When Crane walked back to where she was lying in the grass he saw that Yorke's last bullet had been fired at her. There was a gaping hole in her throat and bubbling noises were coming from her. Out of all those who had been in some way involved in the raid at Sour Creek, Goss was still alive somewhere, Bob Teech, too, though likely with a broken skull; and maybe, if they had got the train moving again, Royce Praeger would be travelling on, looking forward to his cut of the money.

Crane was bone weary. Every muscle in his body was aching. Yet somehow he must get the dead loaded in the wagon and taken into Morland and then begin sending some telegrams. But on the way to Morland, he would pause and place among the less reputable dead, US Deputy Marshal Edward Stoddart, and eventually he would see to it that the old man was buried with due honours.

And then he, Crane, would begin the long, long journey home. To Delia.

This Large Print Book for the Partially sighted, who cannot read normal print, is published under the auspices of

THE ULVERSCROFT FOUNDATION

THE ULVERSCROFT FOUNDATION

. . . we hope that you have enjoyed this Large Print Book. Please think for a moment about those people who have worse eyesight problems than you . . . and are unable to even read or enjoy Large Print, without great difficulty.

You can help them by sending a donation, large or small to:

**The Ulverscroft Foundation,
1, The Green, Bradgate Road,
Anstey, Leicestershire, LE7 7FU,
England.**

or request a copy of our brochure for more details.

The Foundation will use all your help to assist those people who are handicapped by various sight problems and need special attention.

Thank you very much for your help.

Other DALES Western Titles In Large Print

ELLIOT CONWAY
The Dude

JOHN KILGORE
Man From Cherokee Strip

J. T. EDSON
Buffalo Are Coming

ELLIOT LONG
Savage Land

HAL MORGAN
The Ghost Of Windy Ridge

NELSON NYE
Saddle Bow Slim